USA TODAY Bestselling Author

B.J. DANIELS

CARDWELL RANCH TRESPASSER

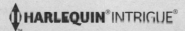

This book is dedicated to my editor, Denise Zaza, and all the readers who didn't want to leave the "canyon" and Cardwell Ranch. Thanks for talking me into this.

ISBN-13: 978-0-373-69680-2

Recycling programs for this product may not exist in your area.

CARDWELL RANCH TRESPASSER

Copyright © 2013 by Barbara Heinlein

Printed in U.S.A.

www.Harlequin.com

ABOUT THE AUTHOR

USA TODAY bestselling author B.J. Daniels wrote her first book after a career as an award-winning newspaper journalist and author of thirty-seven published short stories. That first book, *Odd Man Out*, received a four-and-a-half-star review from *RT Book Reviews* and went on to be nominated for Best Intrigue that year. Since then, she has won numerous awards, including a career achievement award for romantic suspense and many nominations and awards for best book.

Daniels lives in Montana with her husband, Parker, and two springer spaniels, Spot and Jem. When she isn't writing, she snowboards, camps, boats and plays tennis. Daniels is a member of Mystery Writers of America, Sisters in Crime, International Thriller Writers, Kiss of Death and Romance Writers of America.

To contact her, write to B.J. Daniels, P.O. Box 1173, Malta, MT 59538, or email her at bjdaniels@mtintouch.net. Check out her website, www.bjdaniels.com.

Books by B.J. Daniels

HARLEQUIN INTRIGUE

897—CRIME SCENE AT CARDWELL RANCH
996—SECRET OF DEADMAN'S COULEE*
1002—THE NEW DEPUTY IN TOWN*
1024—THE MYSTERY MAN OF WHITEHORSE*
1030—CLASSIFIED CHRISTMAS*
1053—MATCHMAKING WITH A MISSION*
1059—SECOND CHANCE COWBOY*
1083—MONTANA ROYALTY*
1125—SHOTGUN BRIDE‡
1131—HUNTING DOWN THE HORSEMAN‡
1137—BIG SKY DYNASTY‡
1155—SMOKIN' SIX-SHOOTER‡
1161—ONE HOT FORTY-FIVE‡
1198—GUN-SHY BRIDE**
1204—HITCHED!**
1210—TWELVE-GAUGE GUARDIAN**
1234—BOOTS AND BULLETS‡‡
1240—HIGH-CALIBER CHRISTMAS‡‡
1246—WINCHESTER CHRISTMAS WEDDING^
1276—BRANDED†
1282—LASSOED†
1288—RUSTLED†
1294—STAMPEDED†
1335—CORRALLED†
1353—WRANGLED†
1377—JUSTICE AT CARDWELL RANCH
1413—CARDWELL RANCH TRESPASSER

*Whitehorse, Montana
‡Whitehorse, Montana: The Corbetts
**Whitehorse, Montana: Winchester Ranch
‡‡Whitehorse, Montana: Winchester Ranch Reloaded
†Whitehorse, Montana: Chisholm Cattle Company

Other titles by this author available in ebook format.

CAST OF CHARACTERS

Deputy Marshal Colt Dawson—He would have done anything to get close to the owner of the sewing shop. Even risk his life to save her.

Hilde Jacobson—The owner of Needles and Pins suspected something was wrong the moment she met her best friend's cousin.

Dana Cardwell—She had no idea what she was getting into when she discovered a cousin she didn't know she had–and invited her to Montana.

Hud Cardwell—The marshal, glad to see his wife so happy, missed what was really going on.

Dee Anna Justice—The woman who had taken her roommate's identity thought her luck had changed when the invitation came to visit Montana and a cousin she'd never met.

Rick Cameron—He should have known how dangerous it could be when he followed "Dee" to Montana.

Chapter One

Just inside the door, she stopped to take a look around the apartment to make sure she hadn't forgotten anything. This place, like all the others she'd lived in, held no special sentimental value for her. Neither would the next one, she thought. She'd learned a long time ago not to get too attached to anything.

The knock on the other side of the door startled her. She froze, careful not to make a sound. The building super, Mr. McNally, again, wanting the back rent? She should have left earlier.

Another knock. She thought about waiting him out, but her taxi was already downstairs. She would have to talk her way out of the building. It wasn't as if this was the first time she'd found herself in a spot like this.

She opened the door, ready to do whatever it took to reach her taxi.

It wasn't Mr. McNally.

A courier stood holding a manila envelope, a clipboard and a pen.

"Dee Anna Justice?" he asked.

She looked from him to the envelope in his hand. It looked legal. Maybe some rich uncle had died and left Dee Anna a fortune.

"Yes?"

He glanced past her into the empty apartment. She'd sold all the furniture and anything else that wasn't nailed down. Seeing him judging her living conditions, she pulled the door closed behind her. He didn't know her. How dare he? He had no idea what kind of woman she was, and he certainly wasn't going to judge her by the mess she'd left in the apartment.

She cocked a brow at him, waiting.

"I need to see some identification," he said.

Of course he did. It was all she could do not to smile. Well, sneer, as she produced a driver's license in the name of Dee Anna Justice. She'd known where to get a fake ID since she was fourteen.

He shifted on his feet and finally held the pen out to her and showed her where to sign.

She wrote *Dee Anna Justice* the way she'd seen her former roommate do it dozens of times, and held out her hand impatiently for the envelope, hoping there was money inside. She was due for some good news. Otherwise the envelope and its contents would end up with the rest of the trash inside the apartment.

"Thanks a lot," she said sarcastically, as the courier finally handed it over. She was anxious to rip into it right there, but she really needed to get out of here.

It wasn't until she was in the backseat of the cab, headed for the train, that she finally tore open the envelope and pulled out the contents. At first she was a little disappointed. There was only a single one-page letter inside.

As she read the letter through, though, she began to laugh. No rich uncle had died. But it was almost as good. Apparently Dee Anna had a cousin who lived on a ranch in Montana. She ran her finger over the telephone number. According to the letter, all she had to do was call and she would be on her way to Montana. With a sob story, she figured she could get her "cousin" to foot most if not all of her expenses.

She had the cabdriver stop so she could buy a cell phone in the name of Dee Anna Justice. After she made her purchase she instructed the driver to take her to the airport, where she bought a first-class ticket. She couldn't wait to get to Montana and meet her cousin Dana Cardwell.

Chapter Two

"You're never going to believe this."

Hilde Jacobson looked up from behind the counter at Needles and Pins, her sewing shop at Big Sky, Montana, and smiled as her best friend came rushing in, face flushed, dark eyes bright. Her dark hair was pulled back, and she even had on earrings and makeup.

"You escaped?" Hilde said. "I don't believe it." Dana didn't get out much since the birth of her twin boys last fall. Now she had her hands full with four children, all under the age of six.

Her friend dropped a packet of what appeared to be old letters on the counter. "I have family I didn't know I had," she said.

Hilde had to laugh. It wasn't that long ago that Dana was at odds with her siblings over the ranch. *Family* had been a word that had set her off in an entirely different direction than happy excitement.

Last year she'd reunited with her siblings. Her sister, Stacy, and baby daughter, Ella; and brother Jordan and his wife, Deputy Marshal Liza Turner Cardwell, were now all living here in Big Sky. Her other brother, Clay, was still in California helping make movies.

"A cousin is on her way to Montana," Dana announced. "We have to pick her up at the airport."

"We?" Hilde asked, looking out the window at the Suburban parked at the curb. Normally the car seats were full and either Dana's husband, Hud, or Stacy would now be wrestling a stroller from the back.

"Tell me you'll go with me. I can't do this alone."

"Because you're so shy," Hilde joked.

"I'm serious. I'm meeting a cousin who is a complete stranger. I need you there for moral support and to kick me if I say something stupid."

"Why would you say something stupid?"

Dana leaned in closer and, although there was just the two of them in the shop, whispered, "This branch of the family comes with quite the sordid story."

"How sordid?" Hilde asked, intrigued but at the same time worried. Who had Dana invited to the ranch?

"I was going through some of my mother's things when I found these," Dana said, picking up the letters she'd plunked down on the counter and turning them in her fingers.

"That sounds positive," Hilde said, "you going through your mother's things." Mary Justice Cardwell had died nearly six years ago. Because it had been so unexpected and because it had hit Dana so hard, she hadn't been able to go through her mother's things— let alone get rid of anything. Not to mention the fact that her siblings had tried to force her to sell the ranch after their mother's death because Mary's most recent will had gone missing for a while.

"About time I dealt with her things, wouldn't you say?" Dana asked with a sad smile.

"So you found something in one of these letters?" Hilde asked, getting her friend back on track.

Dana brightened. "A family *secret!*"

Hilde laughed. "It must be on the Cardwell side of the family. Do tell."

"Actually, that is what's so shocking. It's on the *Justice* side." Climbing up on a stool at the counter, her friend pulled out one of the letters. "My mother had a brother named Walter who I knew nothing about. Apparently he left home at seventeen and married some woman of ill repute, and my grandparents disinherited him and refused to have his name spoken again."

"*Seriously?* That is so medieval," she said, stepping around the counter so she could read over Dana's shoulder.

"This is a letter from him asking for their forgiveness."

"Did they forgive him?"

"Apparently not. Otherwise, wouldn't I have known about him?"

"So you tracked him down on the internet and found out you have a cousin and now she is on her way to Montana."

"Walter died, but he left behind a family. I found one cousin, but there are apparently several others on that side of the family. Isn't that amazing?"

"Amazing that you were able to find this cousin you know nothing about." Hilde couldn't imagine doing such a thing—let alone inviting this stranger to come visit—and said as much.

"It's not like she's a *complete* stranger. She's my

cousin. You know, since I had my own children, I realize how important family is. I want my kids to know all of their family."

"Right," Hilde said, thinking of the six years Dana had been at odds with her siblings. She'd missed them a lot more than she suspected they'd missed her. "I'm sure it will be fine."

Dana laughed. "If you're so worried, then you absolutely must come to the airport with me to pick her up."

"How did you get out alone?" Hilde asked, glancing toward the street and the empty Suburban again.

"Stacy is babysitting the twins, and Hud has Mary and Hank," Dana said, still sounding breathless. It was great to see her so happy.

"How are you holding up?" Hilde asked. "You must be worn out."

Hilde babysat occasionally, but with Stacy, Jordan and Liza around, and Hud with a flexible schedule, Dana had been able to recruit help—until lately. Jordan and Liza were building their house on the ranch and Stacy had a part-time job at Needles and Pins and another one working as a part-time nanny in Bozeman. Mary was almost five and Hank nearly six. The twins were seven months.

"I'm fine, but I am looking forward to some adult conversation," Dana admitted. "With Stacy spending more time in Bozeman, I hardly ever see her. Jordan and Liza are almost finished with their house, but Jordan has also been busy with the ranch, and Liza is still working as a deputy."

"And I haven't been around much," Hilde added, seeing where this was going. "I'm sorry."

"We knew expanding the shop was going to be time-consuming," Dana said. "I'm not blaming you. But it is one reason I'm so excited my cousin is coming. Her name is Dee Anna Justice. She's just a little younger than me—and guess what?" Dana didn't give Hilde a chance to guess. "She didn't know about us, either. I can't wait to find out what my uncle Walter and the woman he married were like. You know there is more to the story."

"I'm sure there is, but let's not ask her as she gets off the plane, all right?"

Dana laughed. "You know me so well. That's why you have to come along. Dee Anna is in between jobs, so that's good. There was no reason she couldn't come and stay for a while. I offered to help pay her way since she is out of work. I couldn't ask her to come all the way from New York City to the wilds of Montana without helping her."

"Of course not," Hilde said, trying to tamp down her concern. She was a natural worrier, though—unlike Dana. It was amazing that they'd become such close friends. Hilde thought things out before she acted. Dana, who wasn't afraid of anything, jumped right in feetfirst without a second thought. Not to mention her insatiable curiosity. Both her impulsiveness and her curiosity had gotten Dana into trouble, so it was good her husband was the local marshal.

For so long Dana had had the entire responsibility of running Cardwell Ranch on her shoulders. Not that she couldn't handle it and two kids. But now with the twins, it was good that Jordan was taking over more of the actual day-to-day operations. Dana could really start to enjoy her family.

"I'll get Ronnie to come in," Hilde said. "She won't mind watching the shop while I'm gone with you to pick up your cousin."

"I have another favor," Dana said, and looked sheepish. "Please say you'll help show my cousin a good time while she's here. Being from New York City, she'll be bored to tears hanging around the ranch with me and four little kids."

"How long is she staying?" Hilde asked.

Dana shrugged. "As long as she wants to, I guess."

Hilde wondered if it was wise to leave something like this open-ended, but she kept her concerns to herself. It was good to see Dana so excited and getting a break from the kids that she said, "Don't worry, you can count on me, but I'm sure your cousin will love being on the ranch. Did she say whether or not she rides?"

"She's a true city girl, but Hud can teach anyone to ride if she's up for it."

"I'm sure she will be. Did she tell you anything about her family?"

Dana shook her head. "I still can't believe my grandparents had a son they never mentioned. Or, for that matter, that my mother kept it a secret. It all seems very odd."

"I'm sure you'll get to the bottom of it. When is she arriving?" Hilde asked, as she picked up the phone to call Ronnie.

"In an hour. I thought we could have lunch in Bozeman, after we pick her up."

Fortunately, Ronnie didn't mind coming in with only a few minutes' notice, Hilde thought as she hung up. Hilde suddenly couldn't wait to meet this mysterious Justice cousin.

DEPUTY MARSHAL COLT DAWSON watched Hilde Jacobson and Dana Savage come out of the sewing shop from his spot by the window of the deli across the street. Hilde, he noticed, was dressed in tan khakis and a coral print top she'd probably sewn herself. Her long golden hair was bound up in some kind of twist. Silver shone at her throat and ears.

Colt couldn't have put into words what it was about the woman that had him sitting in the coffee shop across the street, just hoping to get a glimpse of her. Most of the time, it made him angry with himself to be this besotted with the darned woman since the feeling was far from mutual.

As she glanced in his direction, he quickly pretended more interest in his untouched coffee. He'd begun taking his breaks and even having lunch at the new deli across from Needles and Pins. It was something he was going to have to stop doing since Hilde had apparently started to notice.

"She's going to think you're stalking her," he said under his breath, and took a sip of his coffee. When he looked again she and Dana had driven away.

"I figured I'd find you here," Marshal Hud Savage said, as he joined him. Colt saw Hud glance across the street and then try to hide a grin as he pulled up a chair and sat down.

He realized it was no secret that he'd asked Hilde

out—and that she'd turned him down. Of course Hilde told her best friend, Dana, and Dana told her husband. Great—by now everyone in the canyon probably knew.

The "canyon," as it was known, ran from the mouth just south of Gallatin Gateway almost to West Yellowstone, miles of winding road along the Gallatin River that cut deep through the mountains.

Forty miles from Bozeman was the relatively new town of Big Sky. It had sprung up when Chet Huntley and a group of men started Big Sky Ski Resort up on Lone Mountain.

Hud ordered coffee, then seemed to study him. Colt bristled at the thought of his boss feeling sorry for him, even though he was definitely pitiful. He just hoped the marshal didn't bring up Hilde. Or mention the word *crush*.

Hilde had laughed when he'd asked her out as if she thought he was joking. Realizing that he wasn't, she'd said, "Colt, I'm flattered, but I'm not your type."

"What type is that?" he'd asked, even though he had a feeling he knew.

She'd studied him for a moment as if again trying to decide if he was serious. "Let's just say I'm a little too old, too serious, too…not fun for you."

He knew he had a reputation around the canyon because when he'd taken the job, he'd found there were a lot of young women who were definitely looking for a good time. He'd been blessed with his Native American father's black hair and his Irish mother's blue eyes. Also, he'd sowed more than a few oats after his divorce. But he was tired of that lifestyle. More than that, he was tired of the kind of women he'd been dating.

Not to mention the fact that he'd become fascinated with Hilde.

Hilde was different, no doubt about it. He'd run into her a few times at gatherings at Hud and Dana's house. She *was* serious. Serious about her business, serious about the life she'd made for herself. He'd heard that she had been in corporate America for a while, then her father had died and she'd realized she wasn't happy. That was when she'd opened her small sewing shop in Big Sky, Montana.

Other than that, he knew little about her. She was Dana's best friend, and they had started out as partners in the shop. Now Dana was a silent investor. Hilde also had her own house. Not one of the ostentatious ones dotting the mountainsides, but a small two-bedroom with a view of Lone Mountain. She'd dated some in the area, but had never been serious about anyone. At least that's what he'd heard.

Some people talked behind her back, saying that she thought she was too good for most of the men around the area. Colt would agree she probably *was* too good for most of them.

"Maybe I've changed," he'd suggested the day he'd asked her out.

Hilde had smiled at that.

It had been three weeks since she'd turned him down. He'd had numerous opportunities to date other women, but he hadn't. He was starting to worry about himself. He figured Hud probably was, too, since the canyon was such a small community, everyone knew everyone else's business.

"I thought I'd let you know I might be taking off

some more time," Hud said after the waitress brought him a cup of coffee. Neither of them had gotten into the fancy coffees that so many places served now in Big Sky. Hud had taken off some time when the twins were born and a few days now and then to help Dana.

"Things are still plenty slow," Colt said, glad his boss wanted to talk about work. He and Hud had gotten close since he took the job last fall, but they weren't so close that they could talk about anything as personal as women.

"Dana discovered she has a cousin she's never met. She and Hilde have gone to pick her up. Stacy's babysitting all the kids right now, so I have to get back. I'll be in and out of the office, but available if needed. Dana wants me to teach her cousin to ride a horse. She's going to try to talk Hilde into taking her cousin on one of the river raft trips down through the Mad Mile. I told her I'd do whatever she wants. As long as Dana is happy, I'm happy to go along with it," he added with a grin.

"Wait, Hilde is going on a raft trip?" Colt couldn't help but laugh. "Good luck with that."

"I think there's a side to Hilde you haven't seen yet. You might be surprised." Hud finished his coffee and stood. "Might be a good idea for you to go along on that raft trip," he added with a grin.

As THE PLANE flew over the mountains surrounding the Gallatin Valley, the now Dee Anna Justice prepared herself for when she met her cousin.

She'd been repeating the name in her head, the same way she used to get into character in the many high school plays she'd performed in. She'd always loved being anyone but herself.

"Dee Anna Justice," she repeated silently as the plane made its descent. The moment the plane touched down, she took out her compact, studying herself in the mirror.

She'd always been a good student despite her lack of interest in school. So she knew how to do her homework. It hadn't taken much research on her laptop to find out everything she could about her "cousin" Dana Cardwell Savage.

The photos she'd found on Facebook had been very enlightening. Surprisingly, she and her "cuz" shared a startling resemblance, which she'd made a point of capitalizing on by tying back her dark hair in the plane bathroom.

"Dee Anna Justice," she had said into the mirror. "Just call me Dee."

The man in the seat beside her in first class had tried to make conversation on the flight, but after a few pleasantries, she'd dissuaded him by pretending to read the book she'd picked up at the airport. He was nice-looking and clearly had money, and she could tell he was interested.

But she'd needed to go over her story a few more times, to get into her role, because once she stepped off this plane, she had to be Dee.

"Hope you enjoy your stay at your cousin's ranch," he said, as the plane taxied toward the incredibly small terminal. Everything out the window seemed small—except for the snowcapped mountain ranges that rose into a blinding blue sky.

"I'm sure I will," she said, and refreshed her lipstick,

going with a pale pink. Her cousin Dana, she'd noticed, didn't wear much—if any—makeup. Imitation was the best form of flattery, she'd learned.

"Is this your first time in Montana?"

She nodded as she put her compact away.

"Staying long?" he asked.

"I'm not sure. How about you?" He'd already told her he was flying in for a fly-fishing trip on the Yellowstone River.

"A short visit, unfortunately."

"Dee Anna Justice," she said extending her hand, trying out the name on him. "My friends call me Dee."

"Lance Allen," he said, his gaze meeting hers approvingly.

Any other time, she would have taken advantage of this handsome business executive. She recognized his expensive suit as well as the watch on his wrist. He'd spent most of the flight on his computer, working—his nails, she noted, recently manicured.

She'd known her share of men like him and hated passing this one up. It didn't slip her mind that she could be spending the week with him on the Yellowstone rather than visiting some no-doubt-boring cousin on a ranch miles from town. But the payoff might be greater with the cousin, she reminded herself.

The plane taxied to a stop. "You don't happen to have a business card where I could reach you if I can't take any more of home on the range?" she asked with a breathy laugh.

He smiled, clearly pleased, dug out his card and wrote his cell phone number on the back. "I hope you get bored soon."

Pocketing his card, she stood to get down her carry-on, giving him one final smile before she sashayed off the plane to see if her luck had changed.

HILDE WASN'T SURPRISED that Dana was questioning her impulsive invitation as the plane landed. "What if she doesn't like us? What if we don't like her?"

"I'm sure it will be fine," Hilde said, not for the first time, even though she was feeling as anxious as her friend.

"Oh, my gosh," Dana exclaimed, as her cousin came off the plane. "She looks like me!"

Hilde was equally shocked when she saw the young woman. The resemblance between Dana and her cousin was startling at a distance. Both had dark hair and eyes. The ever-casual ranch woman, Dana had her long hair pulled up in a ponytail. Her cousin had hers pulled back, as well, though in a clip.

All doubts apparently forgotten, Dana couldn't contain her excitement. She rushed forward. "Dee Anna?"

The woman looked startled but only for a moment, then began to laugh as if she, too, saw the resemblance. Dana hugged her cousin.

Hilde had warned her friend that Easterners were often less demonstrative and that it might be a good idea not to come on too strong. So much for that advice, she thought with a smile. Dana didn't do subtle well, and that was one of the many things she loved about her friend.

"This is my best friend in the world, Hilde Jacobson," Dana said, motioning Hilde closer. "She and I started a sewing shop, even though I don't sew, but now

I'm a silent partner and Hilde does all the work. She always did all the real work since she's the one with the business degrees."

"Hi," Hilde said, and shook the woman's hand. Dana took a breath. The woman's hand was cold as ice. She must be nervous about meeting a cousin she didn't know existed. It made Hilde wonder if Dee Anna Justice was ready for Cardwell Ranch and the rest of this boisterous family.

"Let's get some lunch," Hilde suggested. "Give Dee Anna a chance to get acclimated before we go to the ranch."

"Good idea," Dana chimed in. "But first we need to pick up Dee Anna's bags."

"Please call me Dee, and this is my only bag. I travel light."

The three of them walked outside and across the street to where Dana had left the Suburban parked.

"So how far is the ranch?" Dee asked after they'd finished lunch at a small café near the airport.

"Not that far," Dana said. "Just forty miles."

Dee lifted a brow. "*Just* forty miles?"

"We're used to driving long distances in Montana," Dana said. "Forty miles is nothing to us."

"I already feel as if I'm in the middle of nowhere," Dee said with a laugh. "Where are all the people?"

"Bozeman is getting too big for most people," Dana said, laughing as well. "You should see the eastern part of the state. There's only .03 people per square mile in a lot of it. Less in other parts."

Dee shook her head. "I can't imagine living in such an isolated place."

Dana shot Hilde a worried look. "I think you'll enjoy the ride to the ranch, though. It's beautiful this time of year, and we have all kinds of fun things planned for you to do while you're here. Isn't that right, Hilde?"

Hilde smiled, wondering what Dana was getting her into. "Yes, all kinds of fun things."

DEE STARED OUT the window as they left civilization behind and headed toward the mountains to the south. They passed some huge, beautiful homes owned by people who obviously had money.

She tried to relax, telling herself that fate had gotten her here. The timing of the letter was too perfect. But luck had never been on her side, so this made her a little nervous. Not to mention the thought of being trapped on a ranch in the middle of nowhere. She fingered the business card in her pocket. At least she had other options if this didn't pan out.

She considered her cousin. Dana, while dressed in jeans, boots and a Western shirt, didn't look as if she had money, but she drove a nice new vehicle. And was a partner in a sewing shop—as well as owned a ranch. Maybe her prospects were good, Dee thought, as Dana drove across a bridge spanning a blue-green river, then slipped through an opening in the mountains into a narrow canyon. Dee had never liked narrow roads, let alone one through the mountains with a river next to it.

"That's the Gallatin River," Dana said, pointing to the rushing, clear green water. Dana had been giving a running commentary about the area since lunch. Dee had done her best to tune out most of it while nodding and appearing to show interest.

The canyon narrowed even more, the road winding through towering rock faces on both sides of the river and highway. Dee was getting claustrophobic, but fortunately the land opened a little farther down the road, and she again saw more promising homes and businesses.

"That's Big Sky," Dana said finally, pointing at a cluster of buildings. "And that is Lone Mountain." A snowcapped peak came into view. "Isn't it beautiful?"

Dee agreed, although she felt once she'd seen one mountain, she'd seen them all—and she'd seen more than her fair share today.

"Is the ranch far?" She was tiring of the tour and the drive and anxious to find out if this had been a complete waste of time. Lance Allen was looking awfully good right now.

"Almost there," Dana said, and turned off the highway to cross the river on a narrow bridge.

The land opened up, and for a moment she had great expectations. Then she saw an old two-story house and groaned inwardly.

So much for fate and her luck finally changing. She wondered how quickly she would escape. Maybe she would have to use the sick-sister or even the dying-mother excuse, if it came to that.

Just then a man rode up on a horse. She did a double take and tried to remember the last time she'd seen anyone as handsome as this cowboy astride the horse.

"That's Hud, my husband," Dana said with obvious pride in her voice.

Hello, Hud Savage, Dee said to herself. Things were beginning to look up considerably.

Chapter Three

Deputy Marshal Colt Dawson got the call as he was driving down from Big Sky's Mountain Village.

"Black bear problem up Antler Ridge Road," the dispatcher told him. "The Collins place."

"I'll take care of it." He swung off Lone Mountain Trail onto Antler Ridge Road and drove along until he saw the massive house set against the side of the mountain. Like many of the large homes around Big Sky, this one was only used for a week or so at Christmas and a month or so in the summer at most.

George Collins was some computer component magnate who'd become a millionaire by the time he was thirty.

Colt swung his patrol SUV onto the paved drive that led him through the timber to the circular driveway.

He'd barely stopped and gotten out before the nanny came running out to tell him that the bear was behind the house on the deck.

Colt took out his can of pepper spray, attached it to his belt and then unsnapped his shotgun. The maid led the way, before quickly disappearing back into the house.

The small yearling black bear was just finishing a

huge bowl of dog food when Colt came around the corner.

It saw him and took off, stopping ten yards away in the pines. Colt lifted the shotgun and fired into the air. The bear hightailed it up the mountain and over a rise.

After replacing the shotgun and bear spray in his vehicle, he went to the front door and knocked. The nanny answered the door and he asked to see Mr. or Mrs. Collins. As she disappeared back into the cool darkness of the house, Colt looked around.

Living in Big Sky, he was used to extravagance: heated driveways, gold-finished fixtures, massive homes with lots of rock and wood and antlers. The Collins home was much like the others that had sprouted up around Big Sky.

"Yes?" The woman who appeared was young and pretty except for the frown on her face. "Is there a problem?"

"You called about a bear on your back deck," he reminded her.

"Yes, but I heard you shoot it."

"I didn't *shoot* it. I scared it off. We don't shoot them, but we may have to if you keep feeding them. You need to make sure you don't leave dog food on the deck. Or birdseed in your feeders. Or garbage where the bears can get to it." Montana residents were warned of this— but to little avail. "You can be fined if you continue to disregard these safety measures."

The woman bristled. "I'll tell my housekeeper to feed the dog inside. But you can't be serious about the birdseed."

"It's the bears that are serious about birdseed," Colt

said. "They'll tear down your feeders to get to it and keep coming back as long as there is something to eat."

"Fine. I'll tell my husband."

He tipped his Stetson and left, annoyed that people often moved to Montana for the scenery and wildlife. But they wanted both at a distance so they didn't have to deal with it.

As he drove back toward Meadow Village, the lower part of Big Sky, he thought about what Hud had said about a raft trip down the river. No way would Hilde go. Would she?

HILDE HAD BEEN watching Dee Anna Justice on the ride from the airport to Cardwell Ranch and fighting a nagging feeling.

What was it about the woman that was bothering her? She couldn't put her finger on it even now that she was back in the sewing shop—her favorite place to be.

"So what is she like?" Ronnie asked. The thirty-something Veronica "Ronnie" Tate was an employee and a friend. Hilde loved that she could always depend on Ronnie to hold down the fort while she was away from the shop.

"Dee Anna Justice? It's eerie. She looks like Dana. But she doesn't act like her."

Ronnie seemed to be waiting for Hilde to continue.

Hilde weighed her words. Dana was her best friend. She didn't want to talk about Dana's cousin behind Dana's back.

"More subdued than Dana, but then who isn't? She's from New York City and all this is new to her."

Ronnie laughed. "Okay, what is wrong with her? I can tell you don't like her."

"No, that's not true. I don't *know* her."

"But?"

What *was* bothering her about the woman? Something. "I just hope she doesn't take advantage of Dana's hospitality, that's all." Dana had flown her out here and was paying all her expenses, and Dee was letting her. That seemed wrong.

Ronnie was still waiting.

"I don't want her to be a hardship. Dana is stretched thin as it is with four kids, two still in diapers."

"How long is she staying?" Ronnie asked.

"That's just it—Dana doesn't know." Hilde had always thought visitors were like fish: three days and it was time for them to go. But then again, she enjoyed being alone to read or sew or just look out the window and daydream. Dana was more social, even though she'd deny it.

"I'm sure Dana will show her a good time," Ronnie said.

"I'm sure she will since she has already drafted me to help."

After Ronnie left, she was still wondering what it was about Dee Anna Justice that bothered her. She started to lock up for the day when she recalled Dee's reaction to Hud as he'd ridden up on his horse.

Dee had suddenly come alive—after showing little interest in Montana, the canyon or the ranch before that moment.

DEE MOVED RESTLESSLY around the living room of the old ranch house this morning, running her finger along the horns of some kind of dead animal hanging on the wall. Hud had told her, but she'd forgotten what kind.

Last night, while Dana had seen to the kids, Hud had shown her around the ranch. Dee hadn't been impressed with the corrals, barn, outbuildings or even the view. But Hud, who was drop-dead gorgeous and so wonderfully manly, was very impressive. She'd never met a real live cowboy before. It made him all the more interesting because he was also the marshal.

When the tour of the ranch ended, Hud had excused himself and she'd been forced to stay up late talking with her "cousin." Dana had shared stories of growing up here on the ranch.

Dee had made up a sad childhood of being raised by nannies, attending boarding schools and hardly ever seeing either of her wealthy parents. The stories had evoked the kind of sympathy she'd hoped to get from Dana. By the time they'd gone to bed, Dana had been apologizing for not knowing about Dee and saving her from that lonely childhood.

"Ready?"

Dee turned to smile at Hud. He had offered to teach her to ride a horse this morning. Her first instinct had been to decline. She'd never been on a horse in her life and she really didn't want to now. But she loved the idea of Hud teaching her anything.

"Ready," she said past the lump in her throat.

Hud must have seen her reluctance. "I'm going to put you on one of the kids' horses. Very gentle. There is nothing to worry about."

"If you say so," she said with a laugh. "Let's do it."

Hud led the way outside. He had two horses tied up

to the porch railing. She felt as if she was in Dodge City. This was all so…Western.

"Just grab the saddle horn and put your foot in my hands and I'll help you up," Hud said. She did as he instructed, wobbled a little and fell back. He caught her, just as she knew he would. The man was as strong as he looked.

"Let's try that again," he said with a laugh. Behind them, she heard Dana come out on the porch with the two oldest of their children. Dee had forgotten their names.

"Is she going to ride my horse, Mommy?" the little girl asked.

"Yes, Mary, she needs a nice horse since she has never ridden before," Dana answered.

"Really?" The kid sounded shocked that anyone could reach Dee's age and have never ridden a horse.

This time Dee let Hud lift her up and onto the horse. She gripped the saddle horn as the horse seemed to shiver and stomp its feet. "I don't think it likes me," she said.

"Star likes everyone," the girl said.

Dee was glad when they rode away from the house. She'd always found children annoying. It was beyond her why anyone would want four of them.

Once she got used to the horse's movement, she began to relax. The day was beautiful, not a cloud in the sky. A cool breeze blew through the pine trees, bringing with it a scent like none she'd ever smelled before.

"So this is what fresh air smells like," she joked.

"A little different from New York City?"

She laughed at that. "It's so…quiet."

"You'll get used to it. Did you have trouble getting to sleep last night? People often complain it's too quiet to sleep."

She hadn't been able to sleep last night, but she doubted it was from the quiet. Dana had put her in a large bedroom upstairs at the front of the house. When she'd tested the bed, she found it to be like lying down on a cloud. It was covered with what appeared to be a handmade patchwork quilt, the mattress on a white iron frame that forced her to actually climb up to get into it.

The sheets had smelled like sunshine and were soft. There was no reason she shouldn't have drifted right off to sleep. Except for one.

She found herself reviewing the day in small snapshots, weighing each thing that happened, evaluating how she'd done as Dee Anna Justice. She was much more critical of herself than anyone else could possibly be. But she'd learned the hard way that any little slipup could give her away.

"Dana tells me you grew up back East?" Hud asked, clearly just making conversation as their horses walked down a narrow dirt road side by side.

The real Dee Anna Justice had never been exactly forthcoming about her life growing up. But she'd always gotten the feeling that something had happened, some secret that made Dee Anna not want to talk about her life.

She'd found that amusing, since she would put her childhood secrets up against the real Dee Anna Justice's any day—and win hands down, she was sure.

"It wasn't like *this*," Dee said now in answer to his

question. Then she quickly asked, "Did you grow up here? I get the feeling that you and Dana have always known each other."

"My father was the marshal," Hud said. "I grew up just down the road from here. Dana and I go way back." Something in his tone told her that there had been some problem before they'd gotten together. Another woman? Or another man?

Dee made a mental note to see what she could find out from the sister, Stacy. She'd only seen her for a few minutes, but Dee could tell at once that Stacy and Dana were nothing alike. And while the two seemed close, she got the feeling there was some sort of old friction there.

She'd spent her life reading people to survive. Some people were literally an open book. If they didn't tell you their life story, you could pretty well guess it.

Glancing over at the cowboy beside her, she knew he was honorable, loyal and trustworthy. She considered what it would take to corrupt a man like that.

HILDE PUT THE Open sign in her shop window. As she did, she glanced at the deli across the street. She'd gotten used to seeing Deputy Marshal Colt Dawson sitting in that front window and was a little surprised to find someone else sitting there this morning.

It surprised her also that she was disappointed.

She shook it off, chastising herself.

"Colt has a crush on you," Dana had said a few days before. "Hud says he hasn't dated a single woman since he asked you out and you turned him down."

"I'm sure he'll snap out of it soon," Hilde had said.

Colt Dawson could have any woman he wanted—and had. The man was too handsome for his own good. He'd gotten his straight, thick black hair from his father, who was Native American, and his startling blue eyes from his Irish mother. On top of that, he was tall, broad-shouldered with slim hips and long legs, and he had this grin that...

Hilde shook herself again, shocked that she'd let her thoughts go down that particular trail. It was flattering that Colt had asked her out, but she was his age, and he hadn't dated a woman his own age since he'd come to Big Sky, let alone one who was looking for something more than a good time.

As she started to turn away from the front window of her store, she saw the man at the deli's front table get up and leave. Colt Dawson quickly took his place, his blue-eyed gaze coming up suddenly as if he knew she would be standing there.

Hilde quickly stepped back, but she couldn't help smiling as she hurried to the counter at the back of the store.

A moment later the bell jangled as someone came in the front door. Her heart took off like a shot as she turned, half expecting to see Colt.

"Just need some black thread," said one of her older patrons. "It's amazing how hard it is to keep black thread in the house."

Hilde hurried to help the woman. When she looked out the window again, the front table at the deli was empty, Colt long gone.

"Why didn't you go out with him?" Dana had asked her. "What would it have hurt?"

She hadn't had an answer at that moment. But she did now. A man like Colt Dawson was capable of breaking her heart.

DEE HATED IT when the horseback ride ended, even though she could definitely feel her muscles rebelling. She'd insisted on helping as Hud unsaddled the horses and put them in the corral. *Helping* might have been inaccurate. She'd stood around, asked questions without listening to the answers and studied the man, considering.

Back at the house, Dana announced that Hud was going to take care of the kids while she and her cousin went for a hike and picnic at the falls. That is, if Dee wasn't too tired.

She would much rather have taken a nap than go on a hike since she hadn't gotten much sleep last night, but she couldn't disappoint Dana, especially in front of Hud. So she'd helped pack the lunch to the pickup and the two of them had driven out of the ranch and toward what Dana called Lone Mountain.

"So this is the town of Big Sky?" Dee asked a few minutes later. "I thought it would be bigger."

"It's spread out. There is the upper mountain where the ski lifts are, and the lower mountain where the golf course is. Plus a bunch of houses you can't see from the road," Dana told her. "We'll have to take the gondola to Lone Mountain, if you're here long enough. I think you'll like that—the view is nice. And tomorrow I've set up a rafting trip for the three of us."

"Oh, Hud is going?" Dee asked.

"No, he's taking care of the kids. Hilde is going with

us. In fact, she's joining us for the picnic today." She turned onto a narrow road that went past a cluster of houses and businesses before climbing up through the pines. "Yep, there's Hilde's SUV already parked at the trailhead. Hilde is so punctual." Dana laughed. "It's amazing we're best friends since we are opposites on so many things."

Hilde. The best friend. Dee recalled yesterday feeling Hilde watching her a little too closely. Dana was so trusting, so open. Hilde was more reserved and definitely not trusting, Dee thought. Dana parked next to Hilde's SUV, and Dee glimpsed the woman behind the wheel, her brown eyes so watchful.

DANA CHATTERED AWAY on the hike up to Ousel Falls. Hilde dropped behind her friend and Dee. She hadn't been up to the falls in several years and was enjoying the gentle hike through the pines. She could hear the roar of the creek. It was early in the year, so snow was still melting in the shade and the creek was running fast and high.

The cool air felt good. Hilde was wondering why Dana had insisted she come along. She felt like a third wheel. Not that Dee and Dana seemed to be hitting it off. Dee was quiet, nodding and speaking only to say, "Really?" "Oh, that's interesting." And "Huh." Clearly she wasn't finding anything all that interesting in the information Dana was imparting about the area and its history.

Dana stopped to wait for her in a sunny spot not too far from the falls.

At the falls, Dana opened the cooler she'd brought,

and they sat on rocks overlooking the falls to drink iced tea and eat roasted elk sandwiches.

"It's…interesting," Dee said of the sandwich. "I thought you raised beef?"

Dana laughed. "Wild meat will grow on you," she promised. "Hud always gets an elk and a deer each year. We both really like it."

"I'm not sure I'll be here long enough for it to grow on *me,*" Dee said.

This gave Hilde an opening. "So how long *will* you be staying?" she asked.

"I'm not sure," Dee said, and looked to Dana, who appeared shocked that Hilde would ask such a thing.

"As long as she wants to," Dana said.

Dee smiled. "That could definitely wear out my welcome. The more I see of this place, the more I love it here and never want to leave."

"Montana does that to people," Dana said.

"At least this time of year," Hilde said. "You might not find it as hospitable come winter."

"Oh, I don't know." Dee stretched out on the ground and stared up at the blue sky. "I can see myself sitting in front of that huge rock fireplace at the house with a mug of spiked cider, being pretty content."

"A woman after my own heart," Dana said.

Hilde began to clean up the picnic, putting everything back in the cooler before she got up and wandered over to the edge of the falls.

"What has gotten into you?" Dana whispered next to her a few moments later.

"Sorry. I was just curious how long she's planning to stay," she whispered back. "I didn't mean to be rude."

When Dana said nothing more, she glanced over at her. *"What?"*

"You're jealous of my cousin."

"No, that's not it at all." But Hilde could tell there was no convincing her friend otherwise. "Fine, I'm jealous."

"Don't be," Dana said with a laugh. "You're my *best* friend and always will be." She lowered her voice. "Not only that, Dee has had a really rough life."

"She told you that?" Hilde asked, unable to keep the skepticism out of her voice.

"She didn't have to," Dana said. "I could tell. So be nice to her for me. Please?" Hilde could only nod. "I'm going to get my camera and take a photo."

Hilde turned back to the falls, thinking maybe Dana was right. Maybe she *was* jealous, and that was all it was. The roar of the water was so loud she didn't hear Dee come up behind her. She barely felt the hand on her back before she felt the shove.

She flailed wildly as she felt herself falling forward toward the edge of the roaring falls, nothing between her and the raging water but air and mist.

Dee grabbed her arm and pulled her back at the last second.

"I found my camera," Dana called from over in the trees, and turned in their direction. "Look this way so I can get a picture of the two of you." A beat, then: "Is everything all right?"

"Hilde got a little too close to the edge," Dee said. "You really should be careful, Hilde. Dana was just saying earlier how dangerous it can be around here." She put her arm around Hilde's shoulders. "Say cheese."

Dana snapped the photo.

Chapter Four

"I don't think your friend likes me," Dee said once they were in the pickup and headed back to the ranch.

"Hilde likes you," Dana said, not sounding all that convinced. "But I think she might be a little jealous."

"I suppose that's it," Dee agreed. "Well, I hope she accepts me. I feel so close to you. It's almost like we're sisters instead of cousins, you know what I mean?"

Dana readily agreed, just as Dee had known she would. "Hilde is just a little protective."

"A *little?*" Dee said with a laugh. "I think she's worried I will take advantage of you, stay too long."

"Put that right out of your mind," Dana said, as she parked in front of the house. "You're family. You can stay as long as you'd like."

"Hilde has nothing to be jealous of me about," Dee said. "She's beautiful and smart and self-assured and has her own business. She's what I always wanted to be."

"Me, too," Dana said with a laugh.

"Oh, you have even more going on for you," Dee said. "You have Hud. And the kids," she added a little belatedly, but Dana didn't seem to notice. "And the ranch. I bet you were practically born on a horse."

"I have been riding since the time I could walk," Dana said, then fell silent for a moment. "Do you want to talk about your childhood? I don't mean to pry."

Dee realized that she'd sounded jealous of both Dana and Hilde. The truth had a way of coming out sometimes, didn't it? She would have to be more careful about that around both women.

"There isn't much more to tell." Only because the real Dee Anna Justice hadn't been forthcoming about her family. There had definitely been something in her background she hadn't wanted to talk about. But it could have just been that some wealthy people didn't like talking about themselves or their wealthy families.

So now Dee had to wing it, hoping to give Dana enough to make her feel even more sorry for her. "As I told you last night, when I wasn't away at school, my parents were never around. My father traveled a lot. My mother was involved in a lot of charity and social events. I grew up feeling alone and unloved, yearning for what everyone else had." At least the last part was true.

"I'm sorry, Dee. I wish I had known about you. Maybe you wouldn't have felt so alone," Dana said, as she parked in front of the house. "I would have shared the ranch with you."

Dee watched Hud come out onto the porch and thought about Dana's generous offer to share what she had. "Hud mentioned some high country back behind the ranch that has a great view. I'd love to see it. But this is probably a bad time."

As Dana got out, she suggested it to Hud, who said

the kids were napping and he'd be happy to take her if that was what she wanted to do.

"You sure it's not an inconvenience," Dee said.

"Not at all," he said.

She watched as he gave his wife a kiss and felt that small ache in her stomach at the sight.

"I'll help with dinner when I get back," he said to Dana.

"I'll help, too," Dee said, even though she'd never cooked in her life. In New York City it was too easy to get takeout.

She followed Hud to the four-wheeler parked by the barn and climbed on behind him, putting her arms around his waist. He started the motor and they were off. It didn't take long before the house disappeared behind them and they were completely alone.

Dee watched dark pines blur past. The air got cooler as they climbed, the road twisting and turning as it wound farther and farther back into the mountains. She laid her cheek against the soft fabric of his jean jacket and breathed in the scent of him and the mountains.

There were few times in her life that she'd ever felt safe. It surprised her that now was one of them. Hud was the kind of man she'd always dreamed would come along and sweep her off her feet. How could she still believe in happy ever after after what she'd lived through?

Her parents had hated each other to the point where they'd tried to kill each other. Her father… She didn't even want to think about the role model he'd been to his daughter.

And the men she'd met since then? She let out a

choked laugh, muffling it against Hud's jacket. They'd hurt her in ways she'd thought she could never be hurt.

She'd been waiting her whole life for a hero to come along. When she'd seen Hud Savage come riding up, her heart had filled with helium at the sight of him. He looked bigger than life, strong, brave, the first real man she'd ever known.

She held on a little tighter, wishing Hud was hers.

When they reached the summit, Hud stopped the four-wheeler and shut off the engine.

Dee let go of his waist, stretched and climbed off to look out across the tops of the mountains. "This is amazing," she said, actually meaning it. "You can see forever."

"It is pretty spectacular up here, isn't it?"

She tried to imagine living in country like this. It seemed so far away from the noise and filth of the big cities she'd wandered through so far in her life. What must it be like to wake up to this every morning?

Hud began to point out the mountain peaks, calling each by name with an intimacy that plucked at her heartstrings. She could hear his love for this land in his voice. There was nothing sexier than a man who loved something with such passion.

It took all her self-control not to touch him.

"So what are those mountains over there?" she asked, wanting this moment to last forever. She didn't listen to his answer. She just liked the sound of his deep and melodious voice. Desire spiked through her, making her weak with a need like none she'd known. She wanted this man.

"You have a wonderful life here," she said, realizing

she'd never been so jealous of anyone as she was Dana Savage. "It's so peaceful. I can't imagine having the tie to the land that you do. I've moved around a lot. I've never felt at home anywhere." *Until now,* she thought, but she didn't dare voice it.

Like Hilde, she was sure Hud was wondering how long she was going to stay. But she'd never met a man she couldn't charm. Hud Savage would be no exception.

She moved to the edge of the mountaintop and breathed in the day. She'd been telling the truth about her family moving around a lot. Her father couldn't bear to stay long in any one place—even if he wasn't forced to flee town before the law caught up to him. A small-time con man, he worked harder at not working than he would have had he just gotten an honest job.

"I feel as if I could just fly out over the tops of all these mountains," she said, as she freed her hair to let it blow back in the wind. She stuck out her arms, laughing as she laid her head back. The wind felt good. She felt alive. Free.

"I wouldn't get too close to the edge," Hud said, stepping to her. "I don't want to have to explain to Dana how I lost her cousin."

"No, we don't want that," she agreed, as she met his gaze.

"We should get back. The kids will be waking up and Dana will need help with dinner," he said.

Disappointed, she pulled her hair up again and turned to walk back to the four-wheeler. For a moment, she had felt as if he was responding to her.

She hadn't gone but a few feet when she stepped on

a rock, twisting her ankle as she fell. Hud rushed to her as she dropped to the ground with a groan.

"How bad is it hurt?" he asked, frowning with concern.

"I think I just twisted it, but I can't seem to put any pressure on it," Dee said, wincing in pain as she held her ankle. "I've spent my life walking on sidewalks. I don't know how to walk on anything that isn't flat. I'm sorry."

"Don't be sorry. It happens. Can you get to the four-wheeler?"

She made an attempt to put weight on her ankle and cried out in pain. "I don't mean to be such a big baby."

"I'm just sorry you hurt yourself. Here, I can carry you over to the four-wheeler. If it's still hurting when we reach the ranch, Dana will take you over to the medical center."

"Are you sure you can carry me?" she asked. "I'm so embarrassed."

"Don't be. I can certainly carry someone as light as you," he said, lifting her into his arms.

She was quite a bit slimmer than Dana since her *cousin* had delivered twin sons not that long ago. Nice that he'd noticed, she thought. She put her arms around his neck, and he carried her with little effort over to the four-wheeler. She hated to let go when he set her down on the seat.

"How's that?" he asked.

She lifted her leg over the side, wincing again in pain but being incredibly brave. "Fine. Thank you."

"No problem." He got on and started the motor. "Dana is going to have my hide, though."

"I'm sure it will be fine by the time we reach the

house. I don't want to upset Dana or get you into trouble with her. It's already starting to feel better."

Dee wrapped her arms around Hud's waist, leaning against him again as they descended the mountain. She breathed in the scent of him. She would have him. One way or the other.

AFTER THE HIKE to the falls, Hilde was still trembling an hour later back at the shop. The worst part was that there was no one she could tell. The shove had happened so quickly, even now she couldn't be sure she'd actually felt it. And yet, she knew that Dee had pushed her. Was she trying to scare her?

Or to warn her to back off? The shove had come right after Hilde had asked how long Dee would be staying.

The shop phone rang, making her jump. She really was getting paranoid, she thought as she answered. "Needles and Pins."

"Hi," Dana said. "I just wanted to call and tell you what time we're floating the Gallatin tomorrow."

"Dana, I—"

"Do. Not. Try. To. Get. Out. Of. This."

"You don't need me," Hilde said, and realized she *was* sounding jealous. "I really should work."

"I know business is slow right now. Remember? I'm your silent partner. So don't tell me you have to work. Come on. When was the last time you floated the river?"

"I've never floated it."

"*What?* You've never been down the Mad Mile?"

"No, and I really don't think I want to do it now

when the river is so high. Dana, are you sure this is a good idea?"

"I've already talked to Dee. She's excited. She was trying to get Hud to go with us. Stacy said she'd watch the kids, since Hud said he had something he had to do. Dee was excited to hear you were going with us."

I'll just bet she was.

"Come on. It's going to be fun. You need a thrill or two in your life."

"Don't I, though." What could she say? That there was something not quite right about Dee Anna Justice? That the woman had shoved her at the top of the falls? But then grabbed her to "save" her?

"Great," Dana was saying. "We'll pick you up tomorrow at your place so we can all ride together."

"Great," Hilde said. By the time she hung up, she'd almost convinced herself that Dee hadn't pushed her. That there was nothing to worry about. That she was just jealous. Or crazy.

More likely crazy, she thought, glancing out the front window of the shop hoping to see Colt Dawson. His usual table was empty.

COLT WAS AT the marshal's office filling out paperwork when Hud walked in.

"I would really appreciate it if you would go on this rafting trip with Dana and her cousin this afternoon," Hud said. "Dana's cousin is a little clumsy. Hell, a whole lot clumsy. I don't want her falling off the raft and taking Dana with her."

Colt looked at his boss. "You aren't really asking

me to babysit your wife and her cousin, are you? Why don't you go?"

"I have to take care of a few things at the station. Oh, and I did mention Hilde is going, right?"

Colt swore under his breath. "You think that's going to make me change my mind?"

Hud grinned. "I could make it an order if that would make you feel better."

"You should be worried about Hilde drowning *me*."

His boss laughed. "You'll grow on her over time. Look how you've grown on all of us around here."

"Yeah. What time do I have to be there?"

"You probably better go change." He told him the name of the raft company and where they would be loading in about an hour. "Good luck."

Colt ignored him as he left to head to his cabin. When he'd taken the job, he'd lucked out and gotten a five-year lease on a small cabin in the woods outside of Big Sky. One of the biggest problems with working in the area was finding a reasonable place to live.

At the cabin, he changed into shorts, a T-shirt and river sandals. As he did he wondered what Hilde would have to say when she saw him. He'd never been tongue-tied around women—until Hilde. What was it about her? She seemed unfazed by him. He really didn't know what to do when he was around her.

He knew what he wanted to do. Carry her off and make mad passionate love to her. Just the thought stirred the banked fire inside him.

Colt shook his head, realizing how inappropriate his thoughts were under the circumstances. Hilde hadn't looked twice at him. His chances of getting her to go out on a date with him didn't even look good.

Well, he'd make this float with her and Dana and Dana's cousin because Hud had asked him to keep an eye on them. But he would give Hilde a wide berth. She'd made it clear she wasn't interested. The best thing he could do was move on. Maybe there'd be some young woman on the raft who'd want to go out to dinner later tonight. Best advice he had was to get back on that horse that had thrown him.

With that in mind, he drove down the canyon to where the rafting company was loading the rafts. Dana waved him over as he got out of his pickup. Her cousin stood next to her. He did a double take. The two looked a lot like each other, especially since they were both wearing their hair back. Her cousin was a little slimmer and not as pretty as Dana. There was a hardness to the woman that Dana lacked.

Hilde was standing off to the side, her arms crossed over her chest. He got the feeling she didn't want to be here any more than he did. She wore white shorts and a bright blue print sleeveless top. Her honey-colored hair was pulled up in a way that made her look even more uptight.

He gave her a nod and turned his attention to Dana and her cousin.

"This is my cousin Dee Anna Justice," Dana said.

"Just call me Dee." The woman shook his hand, her gaze locking with his, clearly flirting with him.

"Colt Dawson."

"Colt is a deputy marshal. He works with Hud."

"How interesting," Dee said, still holding his hand.

He didn't pull away. He knew Hilde was probably watching him. Impulsively, he said, "Maybe you'd like to hear more about crime in the canyon at dinner tonight."

"Maybe I would," Dee agreed and looked to Dana.

"Oh, remember? My family is coming tonight for dinner at the ranch so they can meet you," Dana said. "Colt, why don't you come?"

"No, I couldn't. I—"

"I know you don't have other plans," Dana pointed out.

She had him there.

"Hilde's coming, too," Dana said.

He glanced at Hilde. She was studying the ground at her feet, poking one sandaled foot almost angrily at the dirt.

Minutes later, they were all dressed in wet suits and life jackets provided by the rafting company. Dee latched onto his arm as they started to load the rafts, riders sitting three across.

Their guide, though, had him move to a spot on the outside next to an older woman and her husband. In the row directly in front of him, Dee was forced to sit in the middle with Dana on one side and Hilde on the other. Both Hilde and Dana were given paddles.

From where he sat, he could catch only glimpses of Hilde. As their guide shoved the raft off from the shore, everyone on the sides paddled as they'd been instructed. The raft went around in circles for a few minutes before everyone got the hang of it.

Hilde took to paddling as if she'd done it before. The woman was right about one thing. She was serious in most everything she did. He liked that about her and felt like a jackass for having asked Dee out in front of her.

Now they would all be at some family dinner tonight at Cardwell Ranch. He couldn't imagine anything more uncomfortable—unless it was this raft ride.

THE RIVER SWEPT them slowly downstream past huge, round boulders and through glistening, clear green water. A cool breeze stirred the trees along the bank. Overhead, white puffy clouds bobbed along. It was the perfect day for a raft trip.

Hilde tried to relax and enjoy herself, but the memory of what had happened up at the falls made her edgy. She was only too aware of Dee in the seat next to her. She could feel the woman watching her as if measuring her for a coffin. Who was Dee Anna Justice? Not the woman Dana thought she was, that much was clear.

But how was Hilde going to convince Dana of that? Maybe it was better to keep it to herself; after all, Dee would be leaving soon and probably never coming back.

Out of the corner of her eye, she could hear Dana and Dee talking and laughing as the raft picked up speed. Behind her, she was aware of Colt. She'd heard him ask Dee out. Not very subtle, she thought, realizing that she'd hurt him when she'd turned him down for a date. That surprised her.

She tried to concentrate on the river and her paddling. But it was hard with Dee so close and Colt probably watching everything she did. He probably hoped she'd end up in the river.

The Gallatin was known as one of the premiere rafting rivers in the West. The river wound through the narrow canyon with both leisurely waters as well as white-water rapids.

Most of the raft trip so far had been through fairly calm waters, the navigation easy. They'd passed through a few sets of rapids here and there that had had most everyone on the raft screaming as they'd roared through them, water splashing over the raft, Hilde and the other paddlers paddling furiously to keep the raft from turning or capsizing.

But Hilde knew that the rough part was ahead, where they would have to run technical rapids past House Rock for the Mad Mile in the lower canyon.

The Mad Mile was a mile of continuous rapids. The cold water ran fast with huge waves, holes and a lot of adrenaline paddling in the Class IV water. That stretch of river required more precise maneuvering, especially this time of year when the river was higher, and she wasn't looking forward to that.

Hilde noticed that Dee and Dana seemed to be having a great time. She was glad she'd decided not to say anything to Dana. She could almost talk herself into believing that Dee hadn't pushed her at the falls. Almost.

She didn't dare sneak a look back at Colt. She concentrated on her paddling. Not telling Dana was the right thing. It wasn't like Dee was…dangerous.

That thought hit her as the raft made the curve in the river just before the Mad Mile. She could hear Dana explaining about the next stretch of river ahead. Dee actually seemed interested.

They made it through the first few rapids, and the raft passed under the bridge. House Rock was ahead, a huge rock that sat in the middle of the river, forcing the fast water to go around it on each side.

The ride became rougher and wetter with spray coming up and over the raft. There were shrieks and screams and laughter as the raft dipped down into a deep hole and shot up again.

Hilde could see House Rock ahead. It was the other rocks they had to maneuver through that were the problem. The guide picked a line down through the rocks and shouted instructions to the paddlers.

The standing waves were huge. The raft went into the first one, buckling under them. The front of the raft shot down into the huge swell, then quickly upward, stalling for a moment.

Hilde reached with her paddle to grab the top of the wave and help the raft slip over it when suddenly her side of the raft swamped. She tried to lean to the middle of the boat, but Dee was pushing against her. Before she knew what was happening, she was in the water, the top of the wave crashing down on her, the current pulling her under.

As she struggled to reach the surface, Hilde realized she wasn't alone. Dee had fallen out of the raft as well—and she had ahold of Hilde's life jacket. She was dragging her under.

She fought to get away, but something was wrong. She couldn't see light above her. Was she trapped against House Rock? She'd heard about kayakers getting caught against the rock and almost drowning.

But she wasn't against a rock. She was rushing downriver through the huge rapids—trapped under the raft. Somehow, her life jacket had gotten hooked onto a line under the raft. As she struggled to get it off, she realized Dee still had hold of her. She kicked out at the woman, struck something hard, then worked again to free herself.

She couldn't hold her breath any longer. The weight of the raft was holding her down. If she didn't breathe soon—

Arms grabbed her from behind. She flailed at them, trying to free herself from the life jacket and Dee's grip on her. The life jacket finally came off. She had to free herself from Dee's hold and swim out from under the raft before she drowned.

The darkness began to close in. She could no longer go without air. She felt her body give in to the strong grip on her.

Chapter Five

Hilde came to lying on a large flat rock with Colt Dawson kissing her. At least that was her first impression as she felt his mouth on hers. She coughed and had to sit up, gasping for breath.

She could see where the raft had pulled over downstream. The guide was leaning over Dee, who was lying on the side of the raft. "Dee." It was all she could get out before she started coughing again.

"Dee's all right," he said.

Hilde shook her head and let out a snort. "She tried to drown me." Her voice sounded hoarse and hurt like the devil.

Colt looked at her for a full minute before he said, "She tried to save you and almost drowned."

She shook her head more adamantly. "She was the one who hooked my life jacket on the rope under the raft." Hilde could see he didn't believe her. "It's not the first time she's tried to hurt me. When we were up at the falls, she pushed me."

He seemed to be waiting.

"Then she grabbed me just before I fell."

Colt nodded and she realized how crazy she must sound. But if he had been under that raft with her…

"Is Dana all right?" she asked, looking downriver.

"She's just worried about you."

"And *Dee*," Hilde said, seeing how her friend was clutching Dee's hand.

"She's probably worried about Dee because her cousin almost drowned, and this raft trip was her idea," Colt said. "You apparently kicked Dee in the face."

"Because she was trying to hold me down while she hooked my life jacket to that rope." She could see that he didn't believe her and felt her eyes burn hot with tears. "Colt, you have to believe me—there is something wrong with her cousin. I was under that raft with her. She wouldn't let go of me. She hooked my life jacket onto that rope. If you find my jacket…" She was trying to get to her feet.

"Hilde, I'm not sure what you think happened under the raft—"

"I don't know why I expected you to believe me," she said angrily. "Especially about someone you have a date with tonight." He reached for her as she stumbled to her feet, but she brushed off his hand. Stepping down through the rocks, she found a place to cross that wasn't too swift. She could hear him behind her.

All she could think about was getting to Dana, telling her the truth about Dee. Dee was dangerous. Dana had to be warned.

She still felt woozy and should have known better, but she made her way downstream toward the raft. Dana was still holding Dee's hand as she approached. The sight angered her even more.

Hilde remembered right before she'd gone into the river. She'd tried to lean back, but Dee was pushing on her, pushing her out of the boat and going with her. There was no doubt in her mind that the woman had tried to drown her.

"She tried to kill me," Hilde cried, pointing a trembling finger at Dee, who lay on the edge of the raft clearly enjoying all the attention she was getting.

"Are you all right?" the guide asked, sounding scared.

"Did you hear what I said?" she demanded of Dana. "Your cousin tried to kill me."

Everyone on the raft went deathly quiet. "She pushed me off the raft, then she pulled me under and hooked my life jacket on the rope underneath the boat. If Colt hadn't pulled me out of there..." Hilde realized she was crying and near hysteria. Everyone was looking at her as if she was out of her mind.

"I tried to help you," Dee said in a small, tearful voice. She touched her cheek, which Hilde saw was black-and-blue. "If you hadn't kicked me I would have gotten you free from under the raft."

"She almost drowned trying to save you," Dana said.

Hilde let out a lunatic's laugh. "*Save* me? I'm telling you she tried to kill me, and it wasn't the first time." She felt someone touch her arm and turned her head to see Colt standing beside her.

"Let me get you off the river and into some dry clothes," he said, his gaze locking with hers. She saw the pleading in his eyes. He thought she was making a fool of herself. No one believed her. Everyone believed Dee. "I'll take care of Hilde," Colt said to Dana. "You make sure your cousin is okay."

Crying harder, she looked at Dana, saw the shock

and disbelief and pity in her eyes. Through the haze of tears she saw all the others staring at her with a mixture of pity and gratitude that it hadn't been them under the raft.

Her gaze settled on Dee. A whisper of a smile touched her lips, before she, too, began to cry. As Dana tried to assure her cousin that Hilde was just upset, that she hadn't meant what she'd said, Colt urged Hilde toward the edge of the river and the vehicles waiting on the highway above it. The guide had apparently called for EMTs and a rescue crew.

"I don't need a doctor," she said to Colt, as he drew her away from the raft. She could feel everyone watching her and tried to stem the flow of her tears. "I don't need you to take care of me."

"But you do need to get into some dry clothes," he said. "My place is close by."

She looked over at him, ready to tell him she had no intention of going to his house with him.

"You can tell me again what happened under the raft," he said.

"What would be the point? You don't believe me." She stumbled on one of the rocks. He caught her arm to keep her from falling. His hand felt warm and strong on her skin.

"How about this? I believe you more than I believe Dee."

She stopped, having reached the edge of the highway, and glared at him. "Then why didn't you speak up back there?"

"Because it's your word against hers, and as upset as you are, she is more believable right now. That's why I stopped you from telling them about what happened at the falls. Come on, I know this EMT. He'll give us a ride."

"I AM SO SORRY," Dana said for the hundredth time since the raft trip.

Dee planned to milk the incident for all it was worth but was getting tired of hearing Dana apologize. Almost drowning had gotten her out of helping with the huge family meal Dana had cooked. It also had Hud hovering protectively over her.

Dana had told all the family members about the mishap on the river as each arrived. Dee noticed that she'd left out the part about her best friend accusing her cousin of trying to kill her.

It would have been amusing except for the fact that Hilde had almost drowned *her*. Hilde had kicked her hard. For a moment, she'd seen stars. She really could have drowned under that raft. She was lucky she hadn't died today.

She'd had to meet all the family before dinner. There was the sister, Stacy, a smaller version of Dana, whom she'd met only briefly before. She had a pretty, green-eyed baby girl named Ella. Dee remembered that because she got the feeling Stacy might be a good resource—even an ally in the future.

Jordan and his wife, Deputy Marshal Liza Cardwell, were nice enough, but both were wrapped up in each other. Newlyweds, Dana had said. Then there was their father, Angus, and their uncle, Harlan. The talk at that end of the table was about the house Jordan and Liza were building somewhere on the ranch. Far enough away that they hadn't been a problem, Dee thought.

Apparently Dana had another brother, Clay. He worked in the movies in Hollywood and seldom came up to the ranch. Another positive. Hud's father, Brick, wasn't well. He lived in West Yellowstone and seldom got down the canyon. That was also good since he was an ex-marshal.

At the sound of a knock at the front door, Dee looked through the open dining room door into the living room. She could make out a dark shadow through the window.

Probably not Hilde or Deputy Colt Dawson, she thought with no small amount of relief. Hilde had come off as crazy on the river earlier. Dana had been shocked by her friend's accusations and torn in her loyalties. Dee had pretended to be hurt, which only made Dana more protective of her.

Hopefully that would be the last they saw of the woman, she thought, rubbing her jaw. It didn't surprise her that Hilde was turning out to be a problem. That first day Hilde had asked too many questions and was too protective of Dana. Not only that, she paid too much attention.

She suspects something is wrong.

Dee had run across a few intuitive people in her life. Best thing to do was get them out of your life as quickly as possible. After what happened on the river today, she didn't think she would have to worry about Hilde again.

She'd seen the moment when Hilde had realized there was nothing she could say to convince Dana that cousin Dee had been responsible for her almost drowning. Blood was thicker than water—didn't Hilde know that? Dee almost laughed at the thought since she and Dana shared none in common. But it didn't matter as long as Dana believed they did.

All the others on the raft had felt sorry for Dee. Everyone agreed Hilde was just upset and confused. They had tried to comfort Dee, telling her she shouldn't feel bad. The bruise on her cheek from where Hilde had kicked her was now like a badge of honor. She'd tried to save the woman—but there was no saving Hilde from Hilde, she thought now with a silent chuckle.

But apparently Deputy Marshal Colt Dawson was determined to try. Nice that he forgot he'd asked her for a dinner date tonight. She hoped she wasn't wrong about him not being at the door. No, he was probably home taking care of poor Hilde.

She'd seen Dana on the phone earlier. No doubt checking on her friend. Dana was so sure that once Hilde calmed down she would realize that Dee hadn't tried to drown her. So far Dana hadn't seemed to have any doubts to the contrary. Dee had to make sure she stayed that way.

Hud got up from the table to go answer the second knock at the door. Dee got the impression that most anyone who stopped by just walked in and didn't bother knocking.

As the door swung open, she felt her heart drop. She stumbled out of her chair and into the living room. "Rick?"

He saw her and smiled. Anyone watching would have thought everything was fine. Dee knew better.

"Rick, what a surprise." She hurried to the door, belatedly remembering to limp only the last few steps.

She'd managed to hurt herself again in the river—at least that was her story. It would get her out of helping Dana with the dishes and the kids.

"I had to come after I got your phone call," he said smoothly. "Are you all right?"

"It's just a sprain," she said, and realized Hud was watching and waiting for an introduction. Before Dee could, Dana joined them.

"Rick, this is my cousin Dana I told you about and her husband, Hud. Rick…Cameron, a friend of mine from back East." She gave Rick a warning look. "We were just sitting down to a family dinner. Tell me where you're staying and I'll—"

"We always have room for one more," Dana said quickly. "Please join us. Any friend of Dee's is welcome."

Rick stepped in, letting the door close behind him as he looked around, amused at her discomfort. "*Dee,* are you sure you're all right? I've been worried about you."

"I'm fine. You really didn't need to come all this way just to check on me." She bit the words off, angry with him for showing up here and even angrier that he didn't take the hint and leave. She hung back with him as Hud and Dana returned to the large family dining room, where everyone else was waiting.

"What are you doing here?" she demanded under her breath so no one else could hear.

"Is that any way to greet an old friend, *Dee?*"

Her mind whirled. How had he found her? Then with a curse, she realized what she'd done. She'd left a change of address so she could get Dee Anna Justice's mail in care of the ranch. That way she'd know quickly if her cover was blown—as well as collect at least one of Dee Anna's trust fund checks.

In retrospect that had been a mistake. She should have known Rick would come looking for her once he realized she'd bailed on him and the apartment. He'd know the real Dee Anna hadn't gone to a ranch in Montana.

"You can't stay," she whispered. "You'll mess up everything."

He smiled at her. "I can't tell you how good it is to see you, *Dee*."

"Stop doing that."

"I set another place for you, Rick," Dana called from the dining room doorway. "Come join us and I'll introduce you to everyone."

Dee had indigestion by the time the meal wound down. Dana had introduced Rick, and he'd seemed to be enjoying himself, which made it worse. She couldn't wait until dinner was over so she could get him out of here. The trick would be getting him out of town.

Rick could smell a con a mile off. The fact that she was going by Dee Anna Justice had been a dead giveaway. He knew she was up to something. He would want something out of this.

She couldn't have been more relieved when dinner was finally over. Fortunately, because of her re-"sprained" ankle, she didn't have to help with the dishes. Rick helped clear the table. She heard him chatting in the kitchen with Hud and Dana.

She was going to kill him.

Finally, Rick said he was leaving and asked Dee if

she felt up to walking him out to his rental car. She wouldn't have missed it for the world.

"You have to leave," she told him outside.

He glanced at the stars sparkling in the velvet canopy overhead and took a deep breath. "This is nice here. A little too hick for me, but the food was good," he said, finally looking at her. "I've missed you. I thought you would have at least left me a note."

"What do you want?"

"You always were good at cutting right to the heart of it. Isn't it possible I really did miss you?"

"No." He hadn't come here for a reunion. If anything, he'd come to blackmail her.

"Look," she said. "I will cut you in, but I need time. I don't even know what there is here yet."

He laughed. "You can call yourself Dee or anything else you like, but remember, I *know* you. You've staked out something here or you would be gone by now. Is it the land? Is it worth something? Or is there family money I'm just not seeing?"

"There isn't any hidden wealth," she said. "I'm just spending a few days here like a tourist while my cousin shows me a good time. She's picking up my little vacation. That's it."

"You're such a good liar. Usually. But I don't get what you could possibly be thinking here. Does Hud have a rich brother I haven't met yet?"

"Rick—"

"You'd better get back into the house," he said, glancing past her. "You really shouldn't be on that bad ankle too long." He chuckled. "Don't forget to limp or you're going to be doing dishes with the women in the kitchen the rest of your little vacation."

With that, he climbed into his rental car and slammed the door. She slapped the window, trying to get him to roll it down, but he merely made a face at her, started the engine and drove off.

She stood in the faint moonlight mentally kicking herself. Rick was going to ruin everything.

"ARE YOU FEELING BETTER?" Colt asked, as Hilde came out of his bathroom dressed in the sweatpants and T-shirt he'd given her.

She nodded. He'd changed into jeans and a T-shirt that molded his muscled body. She'd never seen him in anything but his uniform before. No wonder he was so popular with women.

He handed her a mug of hot chocolate with tiny marshmallows floating in it. He must have seen her surprise.

"My mother used to always make me hot chocolate when I had a hard day in school," Colt said, and grinned shyly. "I thought it might help."

She curled her fingers around the mug, soaking in the warmth, and took a sip. She couldn't help smiling. "It's perfect." She was touched at his thoughtfulness. "I don't believe I thanked you for saving my life earlier."

He waved her apology away. "I'm just glad you're okay. Would you like to sit down?" he asked, motioning to his couch.

She glanced around his cabin. It was simply but comfortably furnished. He'd made a fire in the small fireplace. This time of year it cooled down quickly in the canyon.

The fire crackled invitingly as she took a seat at one end of the couch, curling her feet under her. She'd finally quit shaking. Now she just felt scared. Scared that she was right about Dee. Even more scared that she wasn't. Had she wrongly accused the woman?

Colt seemed to relax as he joined her at the opposite end of the couch. "Why don't you tell me about Dee?"

She hesitated, upset with herself for the scene she'd made earlier. It was so unlike her. No wonder Dana had looked so shocked. She shouldn't have confronted Dee in front of everyone, but she'd been so upset, so scared. She'd almost drowned. If Colt hadn't pulled her out when he had…

"You can tell me how you really feel," he said quietly.

She took a breath. "I don't know anymore."

"Sure you do," he said and smiled. "Follow your instincts. I have a feeling your instincts are pretty good."

Hilde laughed. "After seeing that hysterical woman on the river a while ago?"

"Almost drowning does that to a person."

She studied him for a moment. He was way too handsome, but he was also very nice. He'd saved her life and now he was willing to listen to her side of it. "What if my instincts are wrong?"

"You know they aren't."

Did she? She took another sip of the hot chocolate. It *did* help. Bracing herself, she said, "There's something…off about Dee."

He nodded, urging her to continue.

"I admit I was worried when Dana told me that she'd

asked a cousin she'd never met to come visit. She's paying for all Dee's expenses. That seemed odd to me. But according to Dana, Dee recently quit her job. Add to that, no one knows how long she plans to stay."

"So you thought right away she might be taking advantage of your friend."

Hilde nodded. "After we picked her up at the airport, Dana was telling her all about this area. I noticed that she didn't seem interested. It wasn't until we reached the ranch and she met Hud that Dee perked up."

He nodded but said nothing.

"I know this all sounds so…small and petty."

"Tell me about the day at the falls."

She finished the hot chocolate and put her mug on the table next to her elbow, noticing the bestseller lying open, his place marked halfway through the book. It was one she'd been wanting to read, and she was momentarily distracted to know that Colt was a reader.

"I didn't want to go on the hike, but Dana insisted. I was probably rude. I asked how long Dee planned to stay. Shortly after that I was standing at the edge of the falls. Dana had gone over to the picnic spot to look for her camera, and all of a sudden I felt a hand on my back and a hard shove. Then Dee grabbed me and warned me to be careful, that it was dangerous around here."

"You believed it was a threat."

"I did."

"But you didn't say anything to Dana."

"I was too shocked and—"

"You talked yourself out of believing it."

She nodded. "Also, Dana was enjoying her cousin so much, I didn't have the heart to tell her."

"You feared she wouldn't believe you."

Hilde let out a laugh. "With good reason. She didn't believe that Dee tried to drown me today."

"But you do."

She swallowed, then slowly nodded. "She wasn't trying to save me. I know you find that hard to believe because I tried to fight you off moments later, when you were only trying to save me."

"Why do you think she pushed you at the falls and yet saved you, then today tried to drown you and maybe really did try to save you?"

"I don't know. It makes one of us seem crazy, doesn't it?"

He smiled. "What is it you think she wants? Dana and Hud don't have a lot money. She can't possibly think she can get her hands on the ranch. She's going to wear out her welcome within a week or so."

"That's just it, I don't know. I just can't get over the feeling that she wants something from Dana. But the more I think about it, the more I feel I must be wrong. What if I'm overreacting? Maybe she *was* trying to save me in the river today."

"Maybe she didn't push you at the falls?"

She looked away. "Dana thinks I'm jealous." She turned to meet his gaze. "Maybe I am." She got to her feet. "I should go home."

Colt rose, too. "What are you going to do?"

"Stay away from Dee," she said with a laugh. "Like you said, she'll wear out her welcome and leave."

"Hud called while you were changing clothes. He's taking Dee up to Elkhorn Lake on a horseback ride tomorrow. Dana's idea. I think we should go."

"*What?* And give her another chance at me?"

He grinned. "That's what I thought. You don't think you imagined any of this. Dee's dangerous, isn't she?"

"Yes. But you're the only person who believes me. Dee always comes away looking like a hero."

"Almost as if she planned it that way. If you really think Hud and Dana are in danger, then I think we need to keep an eye on Dee. Meanwhile, I'll be keeping an eye on you."

Hilde couldn't help but feel a small thrill at the last part. She liked the idea of Colt keeping an eye on her. She told herself not to make anything of it.

"The last thing I want to do is go on a long horseback ride with Dee Anna Justice. What makes you so sure she won't try to kill me again?"

"I can't promise that. But it will look more than a little odd if you meet with yet another accident. I have a plan. But you probably won't like it."

She didn't, but she was so thankful that Colt believed her, she would have gone along with anything he asked.

"Right now, she's won," he said. "You need to throw her off balance and stay close to Dana. There's only one way to do that."

"HE'S A BOYFRIEND, isn't he?" Dana said excitedly when Dee returned to the house after walking Rick out. Hud had apparently gone up to bed. Everyone else had left as she was coming back into the house.

"No, he's..." She saw the sympathy in Dana's expression. Her "cousin" was waiting for some heartbreaking love story. How could she disappoint her with so much at stake?

"Your ex, isn't he." Her cousin drew her over to the couch and patted the cushion, indicating she should sit and spill all. Dee was thankful she had only Dana to deal with now. Dana saw what she wanted to and clearly loved finding a cousin she'd never known she had. Hilde wouldn't have been fooled by her relationship with Rick.

"I can tell he still cares about you," Dana was saying. "He followed you all the way to Montana to make sure you were all right."

Maybe it would be better for everyone to think Rick was a boyfriend, then when she broke up with him and sent him packing, it would play well with the family. It could buy her more time here. She wouldn't want to go back East right away after such a traumatic breakup.

"That's why you quit your job," Dana said. "Did you work with him?"

Why not give her what she wanted and then some? "He was my boss."

"Oh, those kinds of things are so…sticky."

"I knew better, but he was unrelenting."

"I can see that in him. To fly all the way out here."

"I should never have called him and told him where I was. But I knew he'd worry and I certainly shouldn't have mentioned that I sprained my ankle."

"You couldn't know that he'd follow you," Dana said. "He seems nice, though. Is there no chance for the two of you?"

No chance in hell. "He's married," she lied.

Dana looked worried. "Children?"

Dee shook her head. "He and his wife are separated. He's always wanted children, but his wife didn't. She says she doesn't like kids."

Her cousin looked shocked. "Oh, how awful for him."

"Yes. I feel sorry for him, but he needs to try to work things out with his wife."

Dana agreed.

Dee realized she was painting too sympathetic a picture of Rick. "He's been so despondent since I broke it off and..." She lowered her voice. "He's been taking... pills. I'm worried sick he might do something...crazy, between the depression and the drugs. Still I shouldn't have called him to check on him." Like she would have ever called him, but she was grateful that Rick was quick on his feet when it came to lying.

"You did the right thing. Just imagine how you would have felt if you hadn't called and something had happened to him."

"Hmm," she said. "You're right. But maybe I should go back home. I hate bringing my problems to your door."

"Don't be silly." Dana reached out and squeezed her hand. "That's what family is for."

She'd always wondered what family was for. A part of her felt sorry for Dana. The woman was so caring. It must be exhausting.

"You're tired and you've had such an emotional day," her cousin said, glancing at her watch. The fact that Dana still wore a watch and didn't always carry a cell phone told Dee how far from civilization she now was.

"I hope Hilde is all right." She watched Dana's expression out of the corner of her eye, trying to calculate whether or not Dana would call her friend to patch things up or not.

"It's just a good thing Colt was there," Dana said. "He'll take care of her. I'll give her a call later to make sure."

"I feel badly about what she said."

"Don't let it bother you. She was just talking crazy because she was scared. Still, it wasn't like the Hilde I know at all."

She could tell Dana was worried about her friend. "Almost drowning would do that to anyone. I just don't want to come between the two of you."

"You won't. I shouldn't have insisted Hilde come on the raft trip. It really isn't her thing. And anyone would have panicked if they'd been trapped under the raft like that."

"It was just such a freak accident," she agreed.

"I'm sure Hilde realized that, once she had a chance to calm down. I wouldn't be surprised if she shows up tomorrow to apologize."

Don't hold your breath on that one. "I hate to even ask what you have planned for tomorrow," Dee said with a small laugh. She hoped Dana would come up with something away from the ranch with Hud and as far away as possible from Big Sky and Hilde and Rick. "You really are showing me such a great time. How will I ever be able to repay you?"

"It's my pleasure. I thought you'd like to ride up to Elkhorn Lake."

"So you'll be able to go?" she asked.

"No, I have to stay here. Hud is going to take you by horseback, if you're up to it. The lake is beautiful and the trip is really wonderful."

Oh, yes. She couldn't wait.

"I think his deputy Colt is going along."

Dee swore silently. Colt? The man who'd saved Hilde.

"It sounds like fun," she said, although it had sounded much more fun when it was just going to be her and Hud. "I just wish you could go. Maybe next time?"

Dana nodded. "You must come back every year."

Or never leave. "Oh, I would love that."

"Well, sleep tight and don't worry about Rick."

Easy for Dana to say.

Chapter Six

The next morning, Dee got up early and borrowed Dana's pickup to drive into Meadow Village. She still didn't get the town of Big Sky. Everything was so spread out, but it was all close enough that it didn't take her long to find Rick's rental car parked in front of an older motor court motel.

Rick had always been cheap, usually out of necessity because he was broke. She could only guess that that was the case this time.

She had to knock three times before he finally opened the door wearing nothing but a towel wrapped around his waist.

"I wondered when you'd show up," he said with a grin.

She shoved past him into the room. It was pretty much what she expected: bed, television, bathroom. A discount-store piece of so-called art of a mountain from some other state hung on the wall over the unmade bed. Rick's clothes were strewn on the floor and there were a half-dozen empty beer cans next to the bed.

"You always were a slob," she said, turning to look at him. "You have to leave. Now."

"I wish I could, but I spent every dime I had just to get here to see you."

How had she known that was the case? She reached into her shoulder bag. "Here's enough to get you back home and a little extra so you won't starve on the way. The next flight is this afternoon. Be on it." With that she started to leave. "And Rick. No drugs."

"Come on, you know I'm clean. Anyway, you need my help."

She stopped next to him. "No, I don't. I know what I'm doing."

"You and I used to make a pretty good team, as I recall. I'm probably the only person you can truly trust."

"Unless you get drunk or high and shoot your mouth off."

"I've kept your secrets all these years, drunk or sober. Come on, there's a bond between us that not even you can deny." He touched her shoulder.

She pulled away. "I mean it. Don't buy drugs with that money."

"Don't try to kill that blonde woman again."

"I don't know what you're talking about."

"Remember when you and I were little more than kids and I almost drowned? I know you, remember?"

"Then you know to stay out of my business, don't you."

By the time she returned to the ranch, Hud was busy saddling horses. She drove into the yard, but didn't get out of the truck right away. She liked watching him, watching the muscles in his arms and back, imagining being in those arms. Desire hit her like a sucker punch.

She wanted him, and she'd always made a habit of getting what she wanted, any way she had to.

"Best get dressed," Hud called to her, as she climbed out of the truck. "Dana's put out some clothes for you to wear in your room."

She smiled. "Thanks." Inside she went right to her upstairs room. She could hear Dana in the kitchen with the kids. How could the woman stand that noise all the time?

She quickly dressed in the Western attire her cousin had so thoughtfully put out for her, right down to the cowboy boots. Fortunately or unfortunately they were close enough in size that all the clothes fit.

"They're my prebaby clothes," Dana said when Dee came downstairs in them. "I knew they would fit you."

They did, she thought, as she caught a glimpse of herself in the front window reflection. At a glance, she could pass for Dana. A slightly skinnier version, but still…

Dana had made her a breakfast sandwich since she'd apparently missed the usual ranch breakfast. She couldn't believe how these people ate. It was no wonder Dana hadn't gotten back to her pretwins weight.

Breakfast often consisted of pounded and floured fried deer steaks, hash browns, milk gravy, biscuits and eggs. She'd never seen anything like it in her life. There would be changes if she were running this house.

There would have to be a lot of changes. She realized with a start that she hadn't thought this through. Getting Hud would be hard enough. But what to do with Dana and the kids? Dana would have to go. So would the kids. She wasn't interested in having them even come visit on weekends or summers.

She thought of Rick. Maybe he could be helpful after all. She was debating calling him to tell him they should talk, when she looked out and saw with a groan that Hud was saddling *five* horses.

"I see Hud has saddled a bunch of horses," she said nonchalantly to her cousin over the screaming of the children. "Did you decide you could go on the ride with us after all?"

Dana smiled but shook her head. "I need to spend some time with my babies."

"Then Mary and Hank are going?" She was amazed that she finally remembered their names. They were cute kids. If you liked kids.

"No," Dana said with a laugh. "They're too young for this ride."

Just then the front door opened. She turned and was unable to hide her shock as Hilde came in duded out in Western attire. "Hilde?"

"Dee," the young woman said. She hurried to Dee and took both her hands. "I am so sorry about yesterday. Can you ever forgive me?"

Even if she hadn't been good at reading people, she would have seen through *this* apology. But out of the corner of her eye, she saw that Dana was smiling, buying into every word of it. The only gracious thing to do was pretend it was real.

"Hilde, you don't need to apologize, really. I was so scared for you. I'm just glad you're all right. It was such a freak accident."

"Wasn't it, though?" Hilde agreed. "Thank you for

being so understanding. I told Dana I couldn't wait until I saw you to tell you how sorry I was for thinking you had anything to do with my almost drowning."

I'll just bet. "Well, it's good to see you looking so well today. Thanks for coming by."

"Hilde's going on the ride up to the lake with all of you," Dana said.

It took all her effort not to show how that news really made her feel. Hilde was smiling as if she knew exactly what Dee was feeling right now. Apparently such a close call with death hadn't taught Hilde anything.

"That's great," Dee said. "But I would think you'd want to stay home and rest today after what you've been through."

"That's what I told her," Dana said. "But Hilde is tougher than she looks." She smiled and gave Hilde's arm a squeeze.

"I'm not so tough," Hilde said to her friend. "Look at your cousin. She almost drowned yesterday, too, and look how *she's* bounced back." Hilde turned back to her. "Oh, Dee, that bruise on your cheek looks like it hurts. Did I do that?"

"I know you didn't mean to," Dana said quickly.

Ha, Dee thought. "So who else is going with us?" she asked just an instant before Hud came in the door with Colt Dawson right behind him and Rick bringing up the tail end. "Is anyone protecting Big Sky?" Dee asked. "It seems the entire force is right here."

"The other two deputies are holding down the fort," Colt said. "So don't worry about the canyon being safe while we're here with you."

Dee swore silently as Hud asked if they were ready

to go. "I can't wait," she said. Rick was more of a dude than she was. She hoped he got saddle sores.

As they all filed out to the saddled horses, she wondered what the trail was like to this Elkhorn Lake. Hopefully it wasn't too dangerous. She would hate to see anything happen to Hilde. Let alone Rick. Horses were so unpredictable.

Before she mounted her horse, she surreptitiously picked up several nice-sized rocks and stuck them in her pocket.

COLT MADE SURE that he and Hilde stayed behind the others as they rode away from the ranch. He liked riding next to her. It was a beautiful Montana spring day. The air smelled of new green grass, sunshine and water as they followed the creek up into the mountains. Sun dappled the ground as it fingered through the pine branches.

"So tell me about Hilde Jacobson," he said, as their horses ambled along. The others had ridden on ahead, but Colt kept them in sight in case anything happened.

"There isn't much to tell," she said. Then, as if realizing he really was interested, she added, "I grew up in Chicago. My father was a janitor, my mother worked as a housekeeper. I was an only child. My father was determined that I would be the first in his family to go to college."

"And you were?"

She nodded. "I went into business. My father had worked around corporate America and decided that would be the world that I should conquer. I gave it my best shot at least for a while."

"How did you end up in Big Sky owning a fabric store?"

"My father died. My mother told me to follow my heart. I hated big business. I came up here skiing, met Dana and Hud, and the rest is history."

"You and Dana are close, aren't you?"

"We *were.*"

He heard the catch in her throat.

"Your turn," she said after a moment. "Tell me your life story."

"I grew up north of here. I married young. It didn't work out. I went into law enforcement and got the job here."

"You like Big Sky?"

He looked back at the country they'd just left behind and nodded. "It's not as open as I'm used to—the mountains are so much larger—but it grows on you living in the canyon."

"Doesn't it?" she said. "Some people think its paradise and hate to leave."

He saw that she was looking at the two riders ahead of them. Dee was in a deep conversation with Hud. Rick was nowhere to be seen.

DEE WAS LEANING toward Hud and pretending to be fascinated by the different types of rock faces ahead when Hilde and Colt came riding up. Colt cut Hud away from her as slick as the ranch cow dog she'd seen herding calves in the pasture.

A few moments later she found herself riding next to Hilde, also not a coincidence.

"Where's Rick?" Hilde asked, looking behind her. "We seem to have lost him."

"I think he needed to see a tree about a dog. Isn't that what you locals say out here?"

"I'm not a local," Hilde said. "I'm actually from Chicago, and I think it's a dog about a tree."

"Really? I just assumed you were like Hud and Dana, born and raised out West."

"So is Rick from New York City, too? Is that where the two of you met?"

Dee smiled over at her to let her know she knew what she was doing and it wasn't going to work. "I'm still surprised you were up for this ride today after your near-death experience yesterday." She touched the bruise on her cheek. "I know I was still feeling the aftereffects this morning. I didn't realize Montana was such a dangerous place."

"It sure *is*—when you're around." With that, Hilde spurred her horse and rode on up to join Colt and Hud.

So much for that earlier apology, Dee thought with a curse.

She hadn't planned to actually drown Hilde yesterday, but at some point it hadn't seemed like such a bad idea. Dana would have eventually gotten over losing her friend. In fact, she would have needed her cousin even more.

But Dana would have had to lean even more on her husband. Dee had hoped to avoid all of that and just get Hilde to keep her distance. Apparently her plan hadn't worked after the incident at the waterfalls or on the raft trip.

Hilde needed stronger encouragement to get out of

her way. Dee stuck her hand into her pocket, closed her fingers around one of the rocks, hefting it in her hand. Ahead, the trail narrowed as it cut across the side of a rocky mountain face. The horses with Hud, Colt and Hilde fell into single file as they started across the narrow trail.

Dee looked down at the drop-off. Nothing but large boulders all the way down to the creek far below. She let Hilde and her horse get a little farther ahead. She didn't want to be nearby when things went awry.

Poor Hilde. She was having such a bad week. First almost falling off Ousel Falls, then almost drowning in the Gallatin River. Clearly she shouldn't have come along on this ride after what had happened yesterday. She really wasn't up to it.

Dee lifted the rock, measuring the distance. The trail was narrow. If a horse bucked off its rider right now, the rider could be badly hurt—if not killed.

She told herself she had no choice. Hilde had managed to get back in Dana's good graces. Dana was more apt to believe whatever Hilde came up with now. And there was no doubt Hilde would be trying to find out everything she could about cousin Dee.

Reining in her horse at the edge of the pines, she pulled back her arm to throw the rock. All she had to do was hit the back of Hilde's horse. If it spooked even a little, it might buck or lose its footing, and both woman and horse could fall.

Just as she was about to hurl the stone, a hand grabbed her arm and twisted the rock from her grip. She let out a cry of both surprise and pain. Turning in her saddle, she swore when she saw it was Rick.

"Don't be a fool," he said under his breath. "If she has another accident this early, it will only make everyone more suspicious."

"I have to stop her. She's onto me."

Rick shook his head. "I'll help you, but not here. Not today. Be nice to her but watch yourself." He dug into her pocket to pull out the other rocks. "Just in case you get another smart idea while looking at *my* horse's backside," he said, and rode on up the trail to catch up with Hilde.

HILDE KEPT HER eye on Dee during the ride to the lake. But the woman seemed almost subdued after their little talk.

Rick spent most of the time talking with Hud on the last part of the ride up and even when they'd reached Elkhorn Lake. Hilde saw Dee watching the two of them. She got the impression Dee didn't like her boyfriend talking with Hud.

When Hud broke out the lunch Dana had packed, Colt brought her over a sandwich and sat down with her on the rocks at the edge of the lake away from the others.

"Have you noticed the way she is with Hud?" she asked quietly before taking a bite of her sandwich. They'd both been watching Dee.

"Yep."

Hilde locked gazes with him. "I think I know what she's after. She wants Hud."

Colt let out a laugh. *"Hud?"*

"I've been trying to figure out what she wants other than a Montana vacation, all expenses paid."

"She likes to flirt."

"Did she flirt with you?"

He admitted she hadn't except for a few minutes at the river before the raft trip and he suspected that little bit of flirting with him had been for Dana's benefit only. "If Hud's what she's after, then she's wasting her time. He's crazy in love with Dana, not to mention they have four kids together. Hud would never be interested in Dee."

"She wouldn't be the first woman who went after another woman's man."

"Or vice versa," Colt said.

Hilde glanced at him. She knew Colt was divorced. Earlier he'd said he'd married young and that it hadn't worked out. Had another man come after his wife? Or had Colt been seduced away from his marriage?

"But I don't believe any woman can get a man to leave his marriage unless he's willing," Colt added, keeping her from asking him about his marriage. "As they say, it takes two to tango."

"I agree," she said. "Hud would never jeopardize his marriage for a fling with someone like Dee." But had Colt?

"So what's Dee's plan, do you think?" Colt asked quietly. They both watched Dee, who was sitting in a tight circle with Hud and Rick. She was taking tiny bites of her sandwich, clearly not interested in food. Rick had Hud talking, and Dee appeared to be hanging on Hud's every word.

"I wish I knew," Hilde said, feeling a growing desperation as she watched the woman. Dee had wormed her way into Dana's and Hud's lives and she wasn't finished yet. "Now that I know what she's capable of, if I'm right and she is after Hud and she can't get him through seduction, then she will do something more drastic. That's what has me scared."

COLT LOOKED UP from his lunch to study Hilde. She was breathtaking: the sun on her face, her hair as golden as autumn leaves. He was surprised when he'd first come to Big Sky and learned that Hilde and Dana were best friends. They were so different.

Dana was all tomboy. She could ride and rope and shoot as well as any man. Being a mother had toned her down some, but she was a ranch girl born and bred, and she was at home in the great outdoors.

Hilde was all girl, from the clothes she wore to the way she presented herself. He didn't doubt for a moment that she was smart or that she was strong. She could get tough, too, if she had to. He'd seen that the way she'd gone after Dee on the river, but there was something so wonderfully feminine about her. Clearly she enjoyed being a woman.

The combination of smart, strong and ultra-feminine was more powerful than she knew. He suspected it scared away most men.

Dana had told him that Hilde didn't date much. "She must know the kind of man she wants. I just hope she finds him. Hilde deserves someone special."

Colt looked away. He was far from anyone special, but he did wonder what kind of man she was looking for. Or if she was even looking. He thought of his short marriage and the heartbreak it had caused. He'd told himself he would never marry again. But that was before he met Hilde.

They had just finished their sandwiches when there was a splash followed instantly by a scream. He and Hilde turned to look across the lake in the direction the sound had come from and there was Dee swimming in the clear, cold water.

She was laughing and shrieking, but clearly enjoying herself.

Colt noticed that even Hud was smiling at the crazy Easterner.

When it became apparent that she was nude, the men turned around and let her rush out of the water without them watching.

"Did you see that?" Hilde asked.

"I didn't peek."

"Not Dee. Did you see that even Rick turned around? Doesn't that seem odd if the two were boyfriend and girlfriend?"

Colt shrugged. Everything about Rick Cameron seemed odd to him. Add Dee to the mix and you had a rodeo. "She does like attention," he said.

"And she's getting it. Hud isn't completely immune to her. If for some reason Dana wasn't around…"

Colt frowned as Dee came out of the trees dressed again, her hair wet, her face aglow from her swim.

Hud laughed and shook his head when Dee suggested he should have come into the water. No man was completely immune to a woman's attention, especially one who, on the surface, seemed so much like his wife.

Colt had learned that the hard way.

Chapter Seven

After the horseback ride up to the lake, Hilde couldn't wait to get home, shower and curl up in her bed. She hadn't gotten much sleep last night. Add to that everything that had happened to her in the past forty-eight hours and she knew she had good reason to be exhausted.

"Are you sure you don't want to stay and have dinner with us?" Dana had asked. "Hud is going to broil some steaks. I'm making a big salad."

"I would love to, really, but the ride took a lot out of me," Hilde said. She could see that her friend was disappointed, but Hilde had had all the Dee she could take for one day.

She gave Dana a hug, hugging her more tightly than she normally did, afraid for her friend. "Thank you for the offer, though," she said when she let go.

"Once you get to know Dee you'll see how vulnerable and sweet she…" Dana's words died off as she must have seen something in her friend's expression that stopped her.

"Be careful," Hilde said. "I don't want anything to happen to you."

Dana gave her a sympathetic look, and Hilde sensed

that things had changed between them. It made her sad, but she couldn't blame her friend. Dee was like a slow but deadly poison.

"Oh, Hilde, aren't you staying for dinner?" Dee said all cheery, as she came down the stairs. She'd showered and now wore a sundress that accentuated all her assets—which were no small thing. "I know Dana has missed you. I'm afraid she's getting bored with me. I'm not much fun."

"You are plenty fun," Dana said to her cousin. "I could never get bored with you."

"Am I the luckiest woman in the world to have such an amazing cousin?" Dee asked with a too-bright smile. "I'm so glad she found me and invited me to Montana. I'm having a terrific time. I've missed having family so much."

"I know that feeling, so I'm glad," Dana said to her cousin, then turned to Hilde. "Change your mind about dinner."

"Another time." Hilde held Dana's gaze. "Take care of yourself." And she was out the door and headed for her SUV. It was all she could do not to run. She saw Colt glance up from where he and Hud were talking by the corrals. Concern crossed his expression, then his gaze went to the porch where Dee was standing, backlit by the light coming from inside the house.

Dee said something to the two men. Hud laughed and Dee started to come off the porch toward them. Dana called from the kitchen for her cousin. Dee hesitated, clearly disappointed, but went back inside to help Dana.

On the drive to her house, Hilde felt sick to her stomach. She'd never been violent. She was a forget-and-forgive kind of person. At least she thought she was. But for a few moments back there at the house, she'd wanted to walk back to the porch and punch Dee in the face.

"I really need some rest," she told herself, as she parked in front of her house. Once inside, she showered and changed into her favorite silk robe before padding into the kitchen for a glass of warm milk. She knew she couldn't eat anything the way she felt right now.

Back in the bedroom, she finished the milk and crawled into bed with a book she'd been wanting to read—the same one Colt was reading. A book would be the only thing that could get her mind off Dee and her fears for Dana and her family.

She'd read only a few pages, though, when she must have fallen asleep. When the ringing of the phone woke her, she was lying on the open pages of the book, her cheek creased and damp. It took her a moment to realize what had awakened her.

"Hello?" she said, snatching up the phone. Her first thought was that something had happened out at the ranch. Her heart took off like a shot.

"I was afraid you were out with your boyfriend."

She didn't recognize the voice, but her heart was still pounding. "I beg your pardon? I think you have the wrong number." She recognized the laugh, though, and sat up in the bed, trying to shake off sleep. "Rick?"

"One and the same," he said with another laugh. "I've been sitting here having a few drinks, thinking about you."

Hilde groaned inwardly, afraid where this was headed.

"I know your type," he continued. "You like nice

things but you try to hide the fact that you come from money."

She was momentarily surprised by his insight.

"I like nice things, too, but I'm afraid I don't come from money. Far from it." Another laugh. "I'll make you a deal. You want to know the scoop on *Dee?* If you can get your hands on ten thousand dollars, which I have a feeling you can without much trouble, then I will tell you things about dear *Dee* that will make your hair stand on end."

"You sound drunk."

"Not yet."

"Why should I believe you?"

"Because I know she tried to kill you on the river. I'm betting it wasn't the first time she put a scare into you."

"You would sell out your own girlfriend?"

He chuckled. "That's the other thing. *Dee* and I have a complicated relationship. I'll tell you all about it when you get here. How she sold my soul to the devil a long time ago. You'd better hurry before I get too drunk, though. I'm starting to feel the effects of this whiskey." With that he hung up.

COLT WAS AT the marshal's office when the call came in. He saw the dispatcher look in his direction then said she would put the call through to Deputy Marshal Colt Dawson.

The woman on the other end of the line sounded hysterical, and for a moment he didn't recognize Hilde's voice. "Where are you?" he broke in, hoping she would take a breath.

"At the Lazy T Motel, room 9. It's Rick Cameron.

He's dead. She killed him, Colt. She killed him because she knew I was coming here tonight."

Colt wondered why Hilde was going to Rick's motel room, but he didn't dare ask right now. "Step outside the room. Take some deep breaths. I'm on my way." The moment he put down the phone he called Marshal Hud Savage, then he headed for the Lazy T, siren blaring and lights flashing.

Hilde was standing outside, just as he'd told her to. She wore a pair of jeans, a blue-and-tan-print blouse and nice sandals. Her hair was piled on top of her head. Had this been a date?

Jealousy bit into him like the bite of a rattlesnake, filling him with its venom. "What are you doing here, Hilde?" he asked the moment he reached her.

"Rick called. He said he'd tell me about Dee for ten thousand dollars. She killed him. You know she did." The words came flying out, tumbling all over each other.

"Easy," he said and drew her to the side, away from the motel room doors. They had opened, and guests were looking out to see what was going on. "You were going to pay him ten thousand dollars?"

She nodded. "I was asleep when he called. I dressed as quickly as I could."

He had to smile. Only Hilde would grab a matching outfit to come pay off a con man. She'd even taken the time to pull up her long hair into a do that made her look like a model on a runway.

"Stay here, okay?" he said, holding her at arm's length to look into her face. She'd been crying, but she still looked great. As he stepped to the door of the motel, he heard Hud's patrol pickup siren in the distance.

Several more guests stuck their heads out to see what was going on.

"Please go back inside," Colt told them. Inside the motel room he found Rick Cameron sprawled on the bed. There was an empty bottle of whiskey on the floor and an empty bottle of prescription pills under the edge of the bedspread.

He checked for a pulse. Hilde was right. The man was dead. Still when the EMTs arrived seconds later, they attempted to revive him without any luck.

"Looks like an overdose," one of the EMTs told Hud as he came in the door.

Colt stepped out to Hilde, but she'd already heard. "No," she cried, trying to get past him to talk to Hud. "This wasn't an accident. He knew I was on my way over."

The EMTs brought out the body and loaded it into the ambulance. Hud came out after them and walked over to Hilde, clearly unhappy to see her there.

"Dee killed him," Hilde said before the marshal could speak.

Hud raised a brow but didn't respond to the accusation. "I'm going to have to ask you a few questions. Why don't we go down to the office?" He turned to Colt. "Stay here and talk to the motel owner when he gets here."

Colt nodded and didn't look at Hilde as she and the marshal left. The lines had been clearly drawn now. Hud had made that point by telling him to stay there and wait for the motel owner.

He and Hilde were alone on their side of that line, and from Hud's disappointed look as he left, they were on the *wrong* side.

HILDE FOLLOWED HUD in her SUV the few blocks to the marshal's office, her mind racing.

Rick had been ready to tell her the truth about Dee. Surely Hud would realize it was too much of a coincidence for him to overdose right before she got there. She said as much as she followed him into his office.

"I've seen enough of these where the victim mixed alcohol and heavy-duty pain pills. It looks to me like an accidental drug overdose," Hud told her.

"Well, you're wrong." She hated the way her voice broke. Even to her own ears, she sounded close to hysteria. Why wouldn't he believe her?

"Hilde, you're upset. You've been under a lot of strain lately—"

Of course Dana would have told him about her breakdown on the river. "Are you telling me you can't see that people have a lot of accidents around Dee?" she snapped.

"Why don't you tell me how it is that you're the one who found the victim," Hud said, as he settled into his chair behind his desk.

She'd known Hud for years, ever since she'd moved to Big Sky and met Dana. He was like a brother to her. But when he'd sat down behind his desk just then, she saw him become the marshal, all business. She felt the wall come up between them and had to fight tears of frustration and regret.

Taking a breath, she tried to calm down. But she

was at war with herself. She knew he wasn't going to believe her, but at the same time she had to try to make him see the truth.

"I was asleep. Rick called me." She told him about the conversation, recalling as much as she could of it.

Hud nodded when she finished. "You said he sounded as if he'd been drinking. He said he would give you 'the scoop' on Dee. His words?"

"Yes and the way he said 'Dee,' I got the impression she might not really be Dee Anna Justice." She instantly saw skepticism in Hud's expression. No doubt Dana had also told him that she thought Hilde was jealous of her cousin. "There is something wrong with Dee. I feel it."

She quickly regretted blurting it out when Hud said "Hilde" in a tone that made it clear she was too biased against the woman to be credible.

Thank goodness Colt believed her.

"Hud, you have to admit it's suspicious that he calls, ready to tell me about her, and ends up dead."

"You said he sounded drunk. He might have already taken enough drugs to kill him. Which would explain why by the time you got there, he was already dead. Also, you have no idea what 'the scoop' on her might have been. He was a disgruntled ex-boyfriend."

"Was he?" she asked. "All we have is Dee's word on that. I assume she has an alibi?"

"She was at the house. Hilde, she was there all evening."

She knew Dee was behind it. Maybe she'd put something in the bottle of bourbon that was beside the bed. Or hired someone to kill him. But there was no doubt in Hilde's mind that she'd killed him.

"Rick was addicted to prescription drugs," Hud said with a sigh. "Dee said it was one reason she'd broken up with him. She was also worried that he might hurt himself because of the breakup. Apparently she told him after the horseback ride to the lake that they wouldn't be getting back together."

Hilde smiled, not surprised that Dee had covered her bases. Again. "She set that up nicely, didn't she?" she asked, unable to keep the amusement out of her tone.

"Hilde." His voice reeked with impatience.

She got to her feet, giving up. She'd cried wolf too many times without any proof to back it up. No one believed her. Except Colt. If he was telling the truth. She groaned inwardly at the thought that he might just be indulging her because he liked her. Liked her? Or just wanted to get her into his bed because she was a challenge?

"If those are all your questions…"

"Did you see anyone leaving the motel when you drove up?" Hud asked with a sigh.

She shook her head.

"The motel room door was unlocked?"

She nodded.

"Did you hear anyone going out the back as you entered?"

Why was he doing this? He believed it was an accidental overdose. Was he just trying to get her to see that she was wrong? "I didn't see anyone. I really can't tell you any more."

Hud gave her a regretful look. He knew she was angry that he didn't believe her, but there was nothing she could do about that.

"She's after you, Hud."

"Who?" he asked, frowning.

"Dee. She wants *you*."

He got to his feet, angrier now. "Hilde, I don't know what's gotten into you. You of all people know how I feel about Dana, about our family." He shook his head. "Go home and get some rest."

She nodded, seeing that there was nothing more she could say. "If you have any more questions, you know where I live." With that she left.

COLT HAD A pretty good idea how things had gone the moment Hilde answered the door. He'd thought about waiting until morning, but he was worried about her. If things had gone as he suspected they had, she would be upset and might welcome company.

"I just wanted to be sure you were all right."

She shook her head and motioned him inside. "Dee had an alibi. Not that she needs it. No one believes me anyway. She set this up so perfectly, telling Hud and Dana about Rick's drug problem and that she was worried he would do something terrible to himself."

"I'm sorry," he said. "*I* believe you."

"Do you?" She met his gaze with a fiery one of her own. She was good and mad, and she'd never looked more beautiful. He'd only glimpsed this kind of passion in her before tonight. "Or are you just trying to get into my pants?"

He laughed. "As tempting as that offer is, I like to think I have a shot without being forced to lie to you. I believe you, Hilde. It's too much of a coincidence that he should overdose when you're on the way to his motel room. She got to him. I'm not sure how, but she got to him."

Tears filled her eyes. "Why can't Hud see that?"

"Because Dee's good at hiding her true self and Hud operates on proof."

"Colt, I don't even think she *is* Dee Anna Justice."

He raised a brow.

"It's the way Rick called her 'Dee.' I heard him do it on the horseback ride up to the lake. Is there any way to find out if she's even the woman she says she is?"

Colt gave that some thought. He wasn't sure he believed Dee was pretending to be Dana's cousin. He wasn't sure how she could have pulled that off, but he was willing to put Hilde's mind at rest and his own.

"I'll see if I can get her fingerprints. I might need your help."

"You know you have it," she said. "Would you like something to drink? I have some wine."

"You're tired. I should go."

"I could use the company. Just one drink."

He smiled. "If you had a beer…"

"I do."

He followed her through the house to the kitchen. Her house was neat as a pin and nicely furnished. But not overdone. He realized they had that in common: a minimalistic view of the world.

She handed him a beer, poured herself a glass of wine and led him into the living room.

"Dee already told Dana that Rick had been depressed and she was worried about him, since she told him it was over after the horseback ride," Hilde said. "I swear she must have been planning to drug him right from the moment he showed up."

"It's proving it that's the problem," he said. Sitting here in Hilde's house seemed the most natural thing in the world. "I want you to stay away from her unless I am there to make sure she doesn't try to kill you again."

Hilde looked up in surprise. "You can't believe she would try again. She couldn't get away with *another* murder."

"Rick's death will probably be ruled an accidental overdose," he reminded her. "Consider how it would look if something happened to you now. You've been having a streak of bad luck. Plus you've been…over-wrought." She started to object, but he held up his hand. "I'm just saying how Dee would spin it. You got careless, you haven't been yourself. You get the idea. That's why I want you to give the woman a wide berth until she leaves."

"She's not leaving."

"Well, she can't stay forever."

"She can if she finds a way to get Hud all to herself," Hilde said. "I told Hud that Dee was after him."

Colt groaned. "I can imagine how he took that."

"He needed to be warned."

Colt couldn't argue that. He just hoped it wouldn't have the opposite effect and make Hud more sympathetic to Dee.

"She knows we're onto her." Hilde drained her wineglass. "What scares me is what she'll do next. I'm afraid for Dana and her family. If she makes a play for Hud… I have a feeling Dee doesn't take rejection well."

Colt agreed that the whole family could be in danger. "I wish there was some way to get her out of that house."

"I doubt dynamite would work, even if Dana would let you blast her out. Dee has completely snowed Dana."

He could hear her disappointment. "I know it's frustrating seeing Dana and even Hud taken in like this. But you have to admit, Dee is good."

"She's playing this perfectly, too perfectly," Hilde said. "Which makes me think this isn't her first time she's done this."

"Whatever *this* is," Colt said. "I'll see what I can find out about her. Meanwhile, I'll see what we can do about getting her fingerprints." He'd have to be careful. He couldn't let Hud find out that he was investigating his wife's cousin. If Dana wasn't so happy having found a cousin she never knew she had, then Colt was sure Hud would be suspicious of Dee by now.

"I want to help."

"You are going to stay clear of the ranch unless I'm with you. Promise me."

She promised, but he could tell her concern for her friend was weighing heavily on her. What worried him was that if Dee decided to make a move against her, she would use that concern and Hilde would fall right into the trap.

He finished his beer, saw how late it was and got up to leave. Hilde walked him to the door. As he opened it, a cool breeze blew in, ruffling her hair. He reached to tuck an errant golden strand behind her ear like he'd seen her do the few times she'd worn her hair down.

But the moment he did, his hand slid around to the

back of her slim neck. His eyes locked with hers. Her skin felt cool to his touch as he drew her to him.

THE KISS WAS gentle and sweet and so unexpected. Just the touch of his lips sent a jolt through her. Colt must have felt her tremble because he pulled her closer. She could feel his heart hammering under the hard muscles of his chest.

Her lips parted and she felt a rush of heat as he enclosed her in his arms and deepened the kiss.

She felt light-headed. No one had ever kissed her like this. She leaned into him, into the kiss. For the first time in days, Dee Anna Justice was the last thing on her mind.

Colt pressed her against the wall. She could feel the passion in his kiss, in his body. She wouldn't have been surprised if they had made love right there.

Headlights washed over them. Dana pulled in behind Hilde's SUV. They both drew back as if the lights were ice water thrown on them.

"I should go," Colt said. He touched her hand, his gaze locking with hers for a moment. Then he sauntered out to his patrol pickup and drove off.

"Are you all right?" Dana cried. "Hud told me what happened." She turned to look after Colt. "Did I interrupt something?"

"No, it…" She waved a hand through the air. "I'm just glad to see you. Did you want to come in?"

"Just for a moment. I know it's late, but we were out of milk and I couldn't sleep without making sure you were all right," Dana said as she stepped inside. "You've been through so much lately."

"Haven't I," Hilde said.

"You found his body? That must have been horrible."

"You have no idea." She realized she couldn't confide in her once best friend.

"Dee is a basket case."

Hilde tried to hide a smile. "I'm sure she is," she said.

But Dana knew her too well. "Hilde, the man was her *boyfriend*."

"Was he? Or is that just what she told you? Dana, the only thing you know about her is what she's told you. How can you be sure any of it is true?"

Dana stood in the middle of the living room, suddenly looking uncomfortable. "I know you don't like her, but to be this suspicious about everything she says or does—"

"She's playing you, Dana. You told her about the past six years that you didn't have your family because of the fight over the ranch, didn't you?" She saw the answer in her friend's face. "You are so desperate to have family that you're blinded by this woman."

"I don't understand why you're acting like this," Dana said, sounding close to tears.

Hilde tried to stop herself, but she couldn't. She had to tell Dana everything, had to try to reason with her, to warn her.

"She tried to kill me, Dana. At the falls? She pushed me while you were getting your camera, only grabbing me at the last second before I fell."

"Why would she—"

"Because she doesn't want me around you."

"That's crazy," Dana said.

"Yes, it is. And she's living with you and your husband and your children."

They stood only inches apart staring at each other, but Hilde felt as if there was a mountain range between them, one neither of them might be able to climb.

"I'm worried about you, Hilde."

"Really? Because I'm scared to death for you. She killed Rick to keep him from telling me the truth tonight. He'd called me and said he'd tell me Dee's secrets, but I got there too late."

Dana was shaking her head and Hilde saw that her friend was never going to believe her. Until it was too late. "I should go."

Hilde nodded. "Watch her, Dana. I think she's after Hud."

Dana gave her a disbelieving look as if Hilde had finally lost her mind, then she turned and left.

Hilde closed the door behind her and leaned against it. She hadn't even realized she was crying until she tasted the salty tears.

Chapter Eight

"You can't blame yourself for Rick's overdose," Dana said the next morning at breakfast. Hud had left early, called in on some new case. Her "cousin" had been trying to console her. "There are just some people who can't be helped no matter how hard we try."

Dee heard something in Dana's voice. "Like Hilde? I feel responsible for this rift between the two of you as much as I do for what Rick did."

"Don't. Hilde has just been under a lot of strain lately. I didn't realize how much. Then to find Rick like that…"

"So Hilde was the one who found him?" Dee felt her blood pressure rise like a rocket. That bastard. After their horseback ride, he'd threatened to blow her plans out of the water if she didn't include him. "Why would she go over to Rick's?"

Dana looked away to tend to one of the kids. "Apparently he was upset after you broke things off with him again. He called Hilde, wanted ten thousand dollars to tell her things about you."

If she could have killed him again, she would have made this time much more painful. "Why would he do that?" she wailed. "It must have been the drugs talking."

"I'm sure it was."

"So what did he say when she got to his motel room?" Dee asked, trying hard not to let her fear show.

"He was already dead."

Dee tried not to breathe a sigh of relief. "I'm sure he just wanted a shoulder to cry on."

"But to ask her for ten thousand dollars for information about you…" Dana said, and looked at her.

Dee saw the doubt beginning to bloom and knew she had to nip it in the bud and quickly. "I told you Rick had turned to pills," she said, and began to cry again. She'd learned to cry on cue so this was the easy part. "Well, the truth is…Rick had a drug habit. I'm so ashamed."

"You have nothing to be ashamed of," Dana said, quickly coming to her side.

"How could I have fallen in love with a man like him? I didn't know for a long time. Once I realized…I tried to help him. But it was too late. He'd blown all his savings on his habit. It wasn't love that brought him all the way to Montana or me. I was too ashamed to tell you this, but the real reason was to ask me for money. When I turned him down, both for money and his feeble attempt to get me back, I guess he was desperate. He knew Hilde didn't like me…. She was probably ready to give him the money for any kind of dirt on me she could dig up. Oh, Dana, I'm sorry. I know she's your best friend…. See why I feel so badly about all this?"

"But you shouldn't. You haven't done anything. We can't control the way other people react." Dana sounded sad.

"We need to do something to cheer us both up. I would love to go into Bozeman. We could have lunch, maybe do some shopping. What do you say?" She held her breath. She'd seen Hud go off to work this morning and had a pretty good idea that Dana didn't have anyone to take care of the kids. Couldn't really call Hilde, could she? Also, she'd heard Dana promise to make pies with the kids today.

"That sounds wonderful," Dana said. "But I'm afraid it will have to wait." Mary and Hank came running into the room, as if on cue.

"We're making pies with Mommy today," Mary announced.

Dee smiled, but did her best to look disappointed. "As fun as that sounds, Dana, would you mind if I borrowed your truck and went into Bozeman? You probably could use some time alone, and I need to do some shopping."

"Of course. The keys are in the truck. Please help yourself. And when you come back, there will be pie!" Dana laughed as the kids began to cheer noisily.

Dee couldn't wait to leave. "I might take the whole day, then," she said, as she hurried upstairs to get her purse.

COLT CALLED THE shop the next morning right after Hilde opened. "How are you doing?"

She glanced across the street to the deli, half expecting to see him sitting in his usual place. She was disappointed to see that the table was empty. "I'm okay."

"Did you get some sleep?"

"Yes. The wine and you stopping by helped," she admitted.

"Good, I'm glad to hear that. I wanted you to know

that I have to go up to West Yellowstone today on a burglary case."

She could hear the smile in his voice and laughed. "And you thought you'd better remind me that I'm not to go near Dee?"

"Yeah," he said. "Too subtle?"

"I appreciate you thinking of me."

He was silent for a moment before he said, "I've been thinking of you for a long while."

She didn't know what to say, especially since a lump had formed in her throat.

"I wish that kiss hadn't gotten interrupted."

"Me, too."

"How did things go with Dana, or shouldn't I ask?"

"Not well. I know I should have kept my mouth shut, but Colt, I had to warn her. If I put even a little doubt in her mind…"

"You did what you had to. Listen, I probably shouldn't be telling you this. Hell, I *know* I shouldn't. I meant to tell you last night. When we searched Rick, we found three different forms of identification in three different names. We sent his fingerprints to the crime lab in Missoula and we're waiting to see if we get a hit. Right now, we don't know who the guy is."

Hilde felt her heart take off at a gallop. "So there is more to the story. Just like there has got to be with Dee."

"It sure looks that way."

"We have to get her fingerprints."

"Hilde, promise me you won't do anything while I'm in West. You know how dangerous she is. Also…"

She heard him hesitate. "What?"

"She's gone into Bozeman today to do some shopping. She stopped by the office to ask Hud where there was a good place to have lunch. When she heard he's going to be testifying in a trial down there this afternoon, she talked him into having lunch with her."

Hilde never swore so she was as shocked as anyone when a cuss word escaped her mouth. "Even after I told Hud she was after him?"

"You had to be there," Colt said. "She's playing Rick's death to the hilt. She said she needs someone to talk to and has questions that only Hud can answer.... You get the idea."

Unfortunately she did. "We have to get her fingerprints soon."

"I promise you we will. Just be patient. I'll be back tonight. I was wondering if we could have dinner?"

Was he asking her on a date? Or was he just worried about her? "I'd like that."

He sounded relieved. "Good. I could pick you up by seven. I thought we'd go up to Mountain Village, get away for a while."

She felt a shiver of excitement race through her. "I look forward to it." She hung up feeling like a schoolgirl. It was all she could do not to dance around the shop.

Hilde might have let herself go and danced, but the bell over the door jangled and she turned to see Dana's cousin step inside. As Dee entered, she flipped the sign from Open to Closed and locked the door before turning to face Hilde.

"DON'T MAKE A fool of yourself," Dee snapped, as she saw Hilde fumble for her cell phone. Hilde looked so much like a deer in the headlights that Dee had to laugh. "What are you going to tell the marshal? That I came into your shop to try to kill you again? Really, Hilde. You must realize how tiresome you've become."

"Don't come any closer," Hilde said, holding up the phone.

"You're wasting your time. Hud is in Bozeman, Colt is on his way to West Yellowstone—and what's that other deputy's name?"

"Liza."

"Right. She just got a call and is headed up the mountain. By the time any of them get here, I will have unlocked the door and left you safe and as sound as you can be under the circumstances and you'll only look all the more foolish."

"What do you want?" Hilde demanded. But she lowered the cell phone as she stepped behind the counter.

Dee couldn't help being amused as Hilde snatched up a pair of deadly-looking scissors from behind the counter. "You aren't going to use those. Even if you had it in you, everyone would just assume you went off the deep end. You've been teetering on the brink for several days now."

"What. Do. You. Want?" Hilde repeated.

Dee had to hand it to the woman. She was tougher than she looked. "I want you to leave me alone."

"Don't you mean you want me to leave Dana alone?"

"Just let me enjoy this vacation with my family."

"Are they really your family? Rick didn't seem to think so."

Finally. She'd known Rick had shot off his mouth on the phone with Hilde. She'd just needed to know what he'd told her, and apparently Hilde was more than ready to tell anyone who'd listen.

"Rick was on drugs."

"How convenient," Hilde snapped. "He was going to tell me all about you and I have a feeling he knew plenty."

"But ten thousand dollars' worth?" Dee shook her head as she moved closer to the counter and Hilde.

"Dana told you about that?" Hilde didn't sound so sure of herself suddenly.

"She told me everything—how you were convinced that I'd killed Rick—and right before you were finally going to learn all my deep, dark secrets. How frustrating that must have been for you."

Hilde brandished the scissors. "You really don't want to come any closer."

Dee smiled, but stopped moving. "So if I'm not Dee Anna Justice, then who did Rick say I was?" She saw the answer at once on Hilde's face. The woman wasn't good at hiding her emotions. She would never survive in Dee's world. "So he didn't say. You just got the *feeling* I wasn't Dee?" She shook her head. "Yep, you're teetering on the brink. One little push and I'm afraid you're going over the edge. It's going to break Dana's heart. She really does care for you, her *best* friend."

"But you'll be there to pick up the pieces, right?"

"That's what I came here today to tell you," Dee said. "I'm not going anywhere. Accept it. If you don't, I'm afraid of what it will do to you mentally. You seem so fragile as it is."

"You're wrong," Hilde said. "I'm a lot stronger than I look."

Dee didn't expect Hilde to lunge at her with the scissors. It wasn't much of a lunge. Her reaction was to grab Hilde's arm and twist it. The scissors clattered to the floor to the sound of Hilde crying out in pain.

As the shop owner stumbled back, rubbing her wrist and looking scared, Dee bent down and picked up the scissors from the floor by the blades.

"If you're going to try to kill someone, it works better if they don't see you coming at them," Dee said in disgust. As she placed the scissors on the counter, she studied Hilde, realizing she was much closer to the edge of insanity than she'd thought. It wouldn't take hardly anything to push her over.

"I need to get to Bozeman," Dee said. "I have a lunch date with Hud. I suggest you close up shop and get some rest. You might want to see someone about that wrist. I hope it's not sprained. How will you ever explain what happened?" She laughed as she turned toward the door. She almost wished that Hilde would grab up the scissors and come for her again.

At the door, she flipped the sign to Open, unlocked the door and let herself out. When she looked back, Hilde was still standing with her back against the wall, rubbing her wrist. The look in her eyes, though, wasn't one of fear. It was…triumph.

Dee stopped to look again, surprised and worried by what she'd glimpsed in Hilde's eyes just then. Was it just a trick of the light through the window? She couldn't shake the feeling that there was something she was missing. Hilde kept throwing her off balance. The woman was impossible. Anyone else would have taken the hint long before now.

But when she glanced into the shop again, she saw Hilde rush to the door to lock it and put up the Closed sign. Apparently the woman *had* taken her advice and was going to get some rest.

HILDE WAITED UNTIL she saw Dee drive away before she carefully slid the scissors into a clean plastic bag. She was positive she'd gotten the woman's fingerprints because Dee had picked up the scissors by the blades, holding them out as if she wanted to seem nonthreatening.

What a joke. Everything about Dee was threatening.

Once she had the scissors put away, it was all she could do not to call Colt and tell him, but he was working. She would have to wait until dinner tonight since in order for him to run Dee's prints, he would have to do it under Hud's radar. Hilde realized what a chance he would be taking.

Just the thought of Colt made her heart beat a little harder.

He would have a fit when she told him how she'd managed to get Dee's prints. She'd been pretty sure that Dee would take the scissors away from her. She had hoped that Dee wouldn't use them on her, had bet that Dee wasn't ready to kill again. Not yet, anyway. Even if Dee would have claimed self-defense, few people would have believed it.

Well, they wouldn't have believed it before the past few days. Now Hilde wasn't sure what her friends thought of her. That she was mentally unbalanced? That like Dee said, she was teetering on the edge?

Wait until Dee's prints came back. She'd see what they thought then.

What if she is *Dee Anna Justice?* Hilde tried to remember what Dana had told her about Dee Anna and her family. Maybe Dana's grandparents had had a good reason for disinheriting Walter Justice and demanding that his name never be spoken again.

The thought gave her a chill. If there had been something wrong with Walter, wasn't it possible Dee Anna had inherited it?

"No, she's not Dee Ana Justice," she said to herself now. "And I'm going to prove it." If she had a good set of Dee's prints on the scissors. Now she was worried that she might not have.

Hilde started to open her shop when a thought struck her. Dee had gone into Bozeman to have lunch with Hud. That meant Dana would be at the house alone with the kids.

"You promised Colt you wouldn't go near the ranch," she reminded herself, as she went into the back to stuff several plastic bags into her purse. "Colt meant don't go near Dee, not the ranch, and I might not have this opportunity again."

As she started for the door, she realized she was talking to herself. Dee was right. She was teetering on the edge. She was starting to scare herself.

Locking up behind herself and leaving the Closed sign in the window of the sewing shop—something she never did—Hilde headed for Cardwell Ranch.

Chapter Nine

"Dee," Hud said the moment there was a lull in the conversation.

She'd chosen a private booth at the back of the local bistro and had been doing her best to entertain him with fabricated stories about her life.

He'd laughed at the appropriate times and even blushed a little when she'd told him how she'd lost her virginity. Well, how she *could* have lost it if it wasn't for her real life. Her fabricated story was cute and sad and wistful, just enough to pluck at his heartstrings, she hoped. She had Dana where she wanted her. Hud was another story.

She'd noticed that he'd seemed a little distracted when he'd sat down, but she'd thought she'd charmed away whatever was bothering him.

"Dee," he repeated when she'd finished one of her stories. "I have to ask you. How much do you know about Rick?"

The bastard was dead, but not forgotten. She'd been relieved earlier when she'd stopped by Needles and Pins to learn that Rick hadn't had a chance to tell Hilde anything of importance. Had he lived much longer, though, he would have spoiled everything.

"What do you mean?" she asked, letting him know he'd ruined her good mood—and her lunch—by bringing up Rick.

"I found three different forms of identification on him in three different names."

The fool. Why had he taken a chance like that? Because it was the way they'd always done it. So she knew he was planning to start over somewhere else—once he got money from her. If she could have sent him straight to hell at that moment, she'd have bought him a first-class ticket.

"I don't understand." It was the best she could do. Now the marshal would look into Rick's past. It was bound to come out who he really was. Damn him for doing this to her. He really was going to ruin everything.

"Did you suspect he might not be who he said he was?"

She let out a nervous laugh. "He's Rick Cameron. I met his friends. He even had me talk to his mother one time on the phone. She sounded nice."

"I think he lied to you," Hud said gently.

She let him take her hand. His hands were large and strong. She imagined what they might feel like on the rest of her bare skin, and she did her best to look brokenhearted. She even worked up a few tears and was pleased when Hud pulled out a handkerchief and handed it to her.

"Thank you. I don't know what I would have done if this had happened in New York. I have friends there, but at a time like this it is so good to be around *family*." She gave him a hug, but not too long since she felt him tense.

Hilde. The blasted woman had warned him. Of course she had.

"You are so lucky to have such a wonderful family," she said. "Dana is amazing and the kids…what can I say?"

He nodded and relaxed again. "I *am* lucky. And Dana is so happy to have found a cousin she didn't know she had."

"I feel as if I'm wearing out my welcome, though." He started to say something. Not to really disagree, but to try to be polite. "I'll be taking off Saturday. Dana's invited me back for a week next year. I hope she and Hilde regain their friendship. I know it's not my fault, but still…"

Hud smiled. "They'll work it out. I'm just glad you came out to the ranch. You'll have to keep in touch."

"I'll try," she said, furious that between Rick and Hilde, they'd managed to ruin her lunch with Hud and force her to move up her plan—because she wasn't leaving Cardwell Ranch.

WHEN DANA OPENED the door, Hilde saw her expression and felt her heart drop. She thought of all the times she'd stopped by and her best friend had been delighted to see her. Today wasn't one of those days.

"Hilde?" She looked leery, almost afraid. How ironic.

Hilde wanted to scream, *I'm not the one you should fear!* Instead she said, "I bought those ice cream sandwiches the kids like."

Dana glanced at the bag in her hand, but didn't move.

"I won't stay long. I just haven't seen the kids for a few days now. I've missed them."

"Auntie Hilde?" Mary cried and came running to the door. She squeezed past her mother and into Hilde's arms.

She held the adorable little girl close. Mary looked just like the pictures Hilde had seen of Dana at that same age. Was that another reason Dee had been able to fool Dana? Because there was a resemblance between Dana and Dee, one no doubt Dee had played on?

"We're making pies!" Mary announced, as Hilde let her go. "Come on, I'll show you."

Hilde took the child's hand and followed her through the house. Dana had been forced to move out of the doorway, but she looked worried as Hilde entered. What did she think Hilde was going to do? Flip out in front of the kids?

"These are beautiful," Hilde said when she saw the pies. The kitchen looked like a flour bomb had gone off in it. Dana was so good at letting the kids make as big a mess as they had to. She was a great mother, Hilde thought as she looked up at her friend and smiled.

Dana seemed to soften. "Would you like a pie?"

Hilde shook her head. Only a few days ago, Dana would have asked her to stay for dinner and have pie then. Now she seemed anxious that Hilde not stay too long. Dee would be returning.

"We'd better put these in the freezer," Hilde said, handing Dana the bag with the ice cream sandwiches.

"What do you say to Auntie Hilde?"

"Thank you, Auntie Hilde," Mary and Hank chimed in. Dana stepped out on the old back porch to put the ice cream in the freezer.

"I'm taking off now," Hilde called. She said goodbye to the kids, then hurried back into the living room and up the stairs. She assumed Dana had put Dee in the guest bedroom. Hilde had stayed over enough; she almost thought of it as her own.

The door was closed. She opened it quickly and stepped inside. The curtain was drawn so it took her a moment before her eyes adjusted. She knew she had to move quickly.

Dee's cosmetic bag was on the antique vanity. She hurried to it, trying not to step on the floorboards that creaked. Taking the plastic bags out of her purse, she used them like gloves. They were awkward, but she managed to pick up a bottle of makeup, then spied Dee's toothbrush. DNA. She grabbed it, stuffed both into her purse again and hurriedly moved to the door.

Opening it, she stepped out and was partway down the hall headed for the stairs when Dana came up them.

"Hilde?"

"I'm sorry, I just needed to use your bathroom. I hope you don't mind. I drank too much coffee this morning."

Dana relaxed a little. She, of all people, knew about Hilde's coffee habit.

"Thank you for letting me see the kids."

Tears filled her friend's eyes. "I hate this," Dana whispered.

"Me, too. But we'll figure it out. We have to."

Dana nodded, looking skeptical. Who could blame her?

Hilde smiled and touched her shoulder as they passed. She practically ran down the stairs. Dee would realize her makeup and toothbrush were missing. And knowing Dee, she would figure it out.

As Hilde climbed into her SUV, she saw Dana watching her leave. Colt would be furious. He'd realize what was just sinking in for her. Dee had warned her numerous times. The next time they crossed paths, Dee would make sure Hilde Jacobson was no longer a problem.

Hilde just hoped before that time came that she would have the proof she needed to stop Dee Anna Justice—or whoever the woman was.

DEE CALLED STACY after her unsuccessful lunch with Hud. Dana had told her that Stacy had a part-time job as a nanny. Dee was hoping that meant Stacy could get away long enough to talk.

"I was just in town and thought maybe we could have a cup of coffee somewhere," she said when Stacy answered. Dee had gotten her number from the little book Dana kept by the downstairs phone. She'd gotten Hilde's cell phone number out of the book as well.

"Coffee, huh?" Stacy asked.

"Okay, you found me out. I do have some questions about the family."

Stacy laughed. "So you called me. Sure, I know where all the bodies are buried. Do you know where the Greasy Spoon is, off Main Street?"

"No, but I can find it. Ten minutes?"

"I'll have to bring the kids, but they have a play area at the café."

Dee was waiting when Stacy came in with two toddlers: Ella, who she said was now over a year old, and Ralph, the two-year-old she babysat. Stacy deposited the two kids in the play area and came back to sit down with Dee. She could watch the children from where they sat.

"Who names their kid *Ralph?*" Dee asked.

Stacy shrugged and helped herself to the coffee and mini-turnovers Dee had ordered for them. "Named after his wealthy grandfather."

"Then I can see why they love the name," she said and laughed. "I hope I'm not putting you on the spot."

Stacy's laugh was more cutting. "You want to know about me and Dana and Hud, right?"

Dee lifted a brow before she could stop herself. "You and Hud?"

"Dana didn't tell you?"

She lied. "She hinted at something, but I never thought—"

"To make a long story short, Hud and Dana were engaged. I was strapped for money, and truthfully, I was always jealous of Dana. Someone offered me money to drug Hud and get him into my bed so Dana would find him there. It was during a really stupid part of my life. Thankfully my sister forgave me, but it split Hud and Dana up for five years—until the truth came out."

"Wow." Dee hadn't expected this. "Dana mentioned a rift with you and her brothers after your mother died?"

Stacy's laugh held no humor. "We were all desperate for money. Or at least we thought we were. So we wanted to sell off the ranch and split the money. Since our mother's old will divided the ranch between us…"

"But then the new will turned up."

Stacy nodded. "We treated Dana really badly. Family had always meant so much to her… It broke her heart when we turned against her. I will never forgive myself."

"Families are like that sometimes," she said, thinking of her own. "I'm just so glad that Dana found me and I get to be part of yours. I can't tell you how much it means to me."

"Okay, now tell me the big secret with your side of the family." Stacy helped herself to another mini-turnover. "Dana said the family disinherited your father, Walter, because they didn't like who he married? There has to be more to it."

Dee had known Stacy might be more outspoken than her sister. She was a little taken aback by how much. Also, the real Dee Anna Justice had never told her about her father, so Dee was in the dark here.

"I had no idea I had other family," she said. "My father led me to believe my grandparents were dead. Clearly he'd never been close to them."

"And your mother?"

"She's a socialite and philanthropist."

"What?" Stacy cried. "She's not a tramp?"

"Far from it. The woman was born with a silver spoon in her mouth, can trace her ancestry to the *Mayflower* and has more money than she knows what to do with." Dee was offended the family had thought Dee Anna's mother was a skank, even though it wasn't her mother and she didn't like Marietta Justice. The woman was an uptight snob, colder than the marble entry at her mansion. But thanks to her, Dee would be getting her daughter's trust fund check soon.

"So why did the Montana Justice family disinherit his son for marrying wealth?" Stacy asked. "That makes no sense."

No, it didn't. As Stacy said, there had to be more to the story. Dee could only guess. "It's a mystery, isn't it?"

COLT COULDN'T WAIT to get back to Big Sky. He'd been anxious all day and having trouble concentrating on his investigation. It wasn't like him. He took his job seriously. Just like Hilde.

When he'd finally gotten a chance, he'd called Needles and Pins. The phone rang four times and went to voice mail. He doubted she was so busy waiting on a customer that she couldn't answer the phone.

So he waited ten minutes and tried again. Still no answer. He'd never known Hilde not to open the shop. His concern grew even more when he tried later in the afternoon.

He'd finally called Dana and asked for Hilde's cell phone number. "I tried the shop and couldn't reach her."

"That *is* odd," Dana agreed after she'd given him the number. "She stopped out earlier and brought the kids ice cream sandwiches."

Colt swore silently. "How did that go?"

"Okay. But she was acting…strange. Is she all right?"

"She's been through a lot the past few days," he said. "So she didn't stay long?"

"No."

"I'll give her a call and make sure she's all right," he said.

"You'll let me know if…if there is anything I can do?"

"Sure." He quickly dialed Hilde's cell and felt a wave of relief when she answered on the third ring. "You went out to the ranch." He hadn't meant for those to be the first words out of his mouth.

"Don't be mad. I got her fingerprints."

He bit back a curse. "Hilde."

"I know. But she stopped by the shop right after I opened this morning."

If he'd been scared before, he was petrified now. "What did she want?"

"To threaten me. Again. She made it clear that if I didn't back off—"

"So you went out to the ranch and got her fingerprints. I hate to even ask."

"I feel like we are racing against the clock," she said. "I had to do something. She's more dangerous than even I thought."

He agreed. "Okay, just do me a favor. Where are you now?"

"I'm at home. I was too antsy to work today."

"You have the items with her fingerprints on them at the house, right?"

"Yes."

"Okay, just stay there, lock the doors, don't open them for anyone but me. I'm on my way from West. I should be there in an hour. You don't happen to own a gun, do you? Sorry, of course you don't."

"You think you know me that well?" she demanded.

"Yep. Are you going to tell me you do own a gun and know how to shoot it?"

"No."

He laughed. "Go lock your doors. I'm on my way."

DEE WAS DISAPPOINTED when she reached the ranch and found out that Hud was working late at the office. He was the only bright spot in a dreary day.

"I see your ankle is better. That's good," Dana said when Dee came in with the small presents she'd brought the kids. She hadn't wanted to spend much, so she'd found some cheap toys. Mary and Hank thanked her, but she could tell she'd bought the wrong things.

Dinner was just the four of them. Dana had fed the twins and put them to bed. The house was deathly quiet since Mary and Hank were practically falling asleep in their dinner plates.

Dee walked around the ranch while Dana bathed the kids and got them to bed. The night was cool and dark. As she walked, something kept nagging at her about earlier at the sewing shop.

She hadn't been surprised when Hilde had picked up the scissors and lunged at her. Just as she wasn't surprised the woman was slow and uncoordinated, so much so that it had been child's play to take the scissors away from her. Often anger made a person less precise, even clumsy, right?

Coming at her with scissors had seemed a fool thing to do, but Dee hadn't questioned it. Until now.

She recalled how easily it had been to get Hilde to drop the scissors and how surprised she'd been when Hilde had stood there rubbing her wrist as if Dee had broken it.

Hilde hadn't been trying to stab her. Far from it. Then why—

The truth hit her like a ton of bricks.

The scissors.

She swore, stopping in her tracks, to let out her anger in a roar aimed at the night sky. All the pieces fell into place in an instant. The triumphant look in Hilde's eyes.

The woman had gotten her fingerprints!

All the implications of that also fell into place. Once she had her boyfriend Colt run the prints…

Dee slapped herself hard. The force of it stung her cheek. She slapped herself again and again until both cheeks burned as she chanted, "You fool. You fool. You fool." Just as her mother had done.

By the time she stopped, her face was on fire, but she knew what she had to do.

HILDE COULDN'T REMEMBER the last time she was this excited about a date. Well, not exactly a date, she supposed. Dinner. Still she wore an emerald-green dress she'd bought and saved for a special occasion.

Colt's eyes lit when he saw her. "You look beautiful."

She *felt* beautiful.

"I don't think you have any idea what you do to me," he said, his voice sounding rough with emotion. "You make me tongue-tied."

"I really doubt that," she said with a small nervous laugh. The desire in his gaze set her blood aflame.

He took a step to her, ran his fingers along one bare arm. She felt her heart jump. Goose bumps skittered across her skin. His gaze moved over her face like a caress before it settled on her mouth. If he kissed her now—

"We had better go to dinner," he said, letting out a breath as he stepped back from her. "Otherwise…" He met her gaze. "I want to do this right, you know."

She smiled. "I do, too."

"Then we'd better go. I made reservations up on the mountain. It's such a nice night.…"

She grabbed her wrap. Montana in the mountains

was often cold, even in the summer after the sun went down. She doubted she would need it, though. Being this close to Colt had her blood simmering quite nicely.

They didn't talk about Dee Anna Justice or the scissors and other evidence locked up back at the house. Colt asked her about growing up in Chicago. She told him about her idyllic childhood and her loving parents.

"I had a very normal childhood," she concluded. "Most people would say it was boring. How about you?"

"Mine was much the same. It sounds like we were both lucky."

"So your parents are professors at the University of Montana."

"My mother teaches business," he said. "My father teaches math. They'd hoped I would follow in their footsteps, but as much as I enjoyed college, I had no interest in teaching at it. I always wanted to go into law enforcement, especially in a small town. I couldn't have been happier when I got the job here at Big Sky."

He had driven up the winding road that climbed to the Mountain Village. There weren't a lot of businesses open this time of year, but more stayed open all year than in the old days, when there really were only two seasons at Big Sky.

The air was cold up here but crystal clear. Colt was the perfect gentleman, opening her door after he parked. Hilde stood for a moment and admired the stars. With so few other lights, the sky was a dark canopy glittering with white stars. A sliver of moon hung just over the mountains.

"Could this night be more perfect?" she whispered.

When she looked at Colt, he grinned and said, "Let's

see." His kiss was soft and gentle, a brush across the lips as light as the breeze that stirred the loose tendrils of her hair. And then he drew her to him and deepened the kiss, breaking it off as the door of the restaurant opened and a group of four came out laughing and talking.

"We just keep getting interrupted," Colt said with a laugh. He put his arm around her waist and they entered the restaurant.

Hilde had never felt so alive. The night seemed to hold its breath in expectation. She could smell adventure on the air, feel it in her every nerve ending. She had a feeling that tonight would be one she would never forget.

Over dinner, they talked about movies and books, laughed about the crazy things they did when they were kids, and Colt found himself completely enthralled by his date.

Hilde was, as his grandfather used to say, the whole ball of wax. She was smart and ambitious, a hard worker, and yet she volunteered for several organizations in her spare time. She loved nature, cared about the environment and made him laugh.

On top of that, she was beautiful, sexy and a good dancer. After dinner, they'd danced out in the starlight until he thought he would go crazy if he didn't get her alone and naked.

"Is it just me, or do you want to get out of here?" Colt said after they took a break from the dance floor.

"I thought you'd never ask."

He laughed and they left. It was all he could do not

to race down the mountain, but the switchback curves kept him in check.

Once out of the vehicle, though, all bets were off. They were in each other's arms, kissing as they stumbled toward her front door. Once inside, they practically tore each other's clothes off, dropping articles of clothing in a crooked path before making it only to the rug in front of the fireplace.

"Hilde," Colt said, cupping her face in his hands as he leaned over her. He couldn't find words to tell her how beautiful she was or how much he wanted her. Or that he had fallen in love with her. He couldn't even tell her the exact moment. He just knew that he had.

Fortunately, he didn't have to put any of that into words. Not tonight. He saw that she understood. It was in her amazing brown eyes and in the one word she uttered as he entered her. "Colt."

LATER, COLT CARRIED her to her bed and made love to her slowly. The urgency of their first lovemaking had cooled. He took his time letting his gaze and his fingers and his tongue graze her body as he took full possession of her.

Hilde cried out with a passion she'd never known existed as he cupped her breasts and lathed her nipples with his tongue until she felt her whole body quake. She surrendered to him in a way she'd never given herself to another man. His demanding kisses took her to new heights.

And when he finished, his gaze locked with hers, she felt a release that left her sated and happier than she'd ever known.

As he lay curled against her, one arm thrown protectively over her, she closed her eyes and drifted off to sleep feeling…loved.

Chapter Ten

Dee woke from the nightmare in a cold sweat. For a few moments, she couldn't catch her breath. She swung her legs out of bed and stumbled to the window, gulping for air. Her heart felt as if it would pound its way out of her chest.

It was the same nightmare she'd had since she was a girl. She was in a coffin. It was pitch-black. There was no air. She was trapped, and even though she'd screamed herself hoarse, no one had come to save her.

She shoved open the screenless window all the way and leaned out to breathe in the night air. A sliver of moon hung over the top of the mountain. A million stars twinkled against the midnight-blue sky. She shivered as the cold mountain air quickly dried her perspiration and sent goose bumps skittering over her skin.

The nightmare was coming more frequently—just as the doctor had told her it would.

"Do night terrors run in your family?" he'd asked, studying her over the top of his glasses.

"I don't know. I never asked."

"How old did you say you were?"

She'd been in her early twenties at the time.

He'd frowned. "What about sleepwalking?"

"Sometimes I wake up in a strange place and I don't know how I've gotten there."

He nodded, his frown deepening as he tossed her file on his desk. "I'm going to give you a referral to a neurologist."

"You're saying there's something wrong with me?"

"Just a precaution. Sleepwalking and night terrors at your age are fairly uncommon and could be the result of a neurological disorder."

She'd laughed after she left his office. "He thinks I'm crazy." She'd been amused at the time.

But back then she was sleepwalking and having the nightmare only every so often.

Now…

She looked out at the peaceful night. "This is all I need. This place and Hud and I will be fine," she whispered. "Once I get rid of the stumbling blocks, I'll be fine for the first time in my life."

But that was the problem, wasn't it? There were more stumbling blocks than she'd ever run into before. More chances to get caught.

"It would be worth it, though," she said as she heard a horse whinny out in the corrals. All this could be hers. *Would* be hers. She deserved Dana's happiness. She deserved Dana's life—minus the kids.

After getting dressed, she sneaked out and made the walk into town. It was only a couple of miles and she'd walked it before and gotten away with it. If anyone discovered her missing, she'd say she'd gone out to the corral to check the horses. She wasn't worried. So far, they'd believed everything she told them.

THE NEXT MORNING, Colt tried to talk Hilde out of opening the shop. "Can't you have someone else man Needles and Pins for a few weeks?"

Hilde touched his handsome face, cupping his strong jaw, and smiled into those blue eyes of his. He'd been so gentle, so loving, last night when they'd made love. At least the second time. Before that, he'd let his passion run as wild as horses in a windstorm.

Her skin still tingled from the memory. She'd never known that kind of wild abandon. Just the thought thrilled her. She'd awakened feeling as if she could conquer the world. Hadn't she always known that she could be anything she wanted with the right man—in or out of bed?

"I am not going to let Dee or whoever she is keep me from doing what I love," she said, as she felt the rough stubble along his strong jawline. "Especially this morning when I'm feeling so…"

He laughed. "So…?"

"Invincible."

Colt pulled her to him and kissed her. As he drew back, he said, "I love seeing you like this, but Dee will figure out that you have her fingerprints and DNA. She isn't going to take this lying down. You have to know that."

She nodded. "Remember? I know what she's capable of. And I know she isn't finished. How long before we know who she is?" Colt had left for a while before daylight to go to the office to run Dee's fingerprints. He had a friend at the crime lab he'd called.

"You're counting on her fingerprints being on file.

She might not have a record. Also, she might actually be Dee Anna Justice."

Hilde knew Dee was slippery. She might have avoided getting arrested. Might never have had a job that required she be fingerprinted. She might even be who she said she was. But all Hilde could do was hope that not only was she right about Dee being an impostor—but also that the woman had had at least one run-in with the law so her prints would come up. The sooner Dee was exposed, the sooner she would be gone from the ranch.

"I just don't want you getting your hopes up. The toothbrush was a good idea. We might be able to compare Dee's DNA to Dana's."

"I should have thought to get Dana's DNA while I was at it."

"Don't even think about," he said, holding her away from him so she couldn't avoid his gaze. "I'm serious. You have to stay away from Cardwell Ranch."

Hilde nodded. By now Dee would have realized that her makeup and toothbrush were missing. Hopefully she was running scared.

COLT HATED THAT he had to go back down to West Yellowstone on the burglary case today. He didn't like leaving Hilde alone.

"Can I see you for a minute?" the marshal asked, as he was getting ready to leave the office later that morning.

Colt stepped into Hud's office.

"Close the door, please."

He turned to close the door, worry making him anxious. Hud had always run the station in a rather informal way. Not that they all weren't serious about their jobs. But Hud had never seen the need to throw around his weight.

"Have a sit," he said now.

"Is something wrong?" Colt asked, afraid Hud had somehow found out that he'd sent Dee's prints to his friend who worked at the crime lab.

"I wanted to talk to you about Hilde." Hud shook his head. "I know, it's not my place as your boss. Or even as your friend. But I feel I have to. Did you see her last night?"

Colt almost laughed. He figured Hud already knew that his patrol pickup had been parked in front of her house all night. News traveled fast in such a small, isolated community. Gossip was about the only excitement this time of year. It was too early for most tourists or seasonal homeowners, so things were more than a little quiet.

"Yes, I saw her," he said, keeping his face straight.

"I've known Hilde for a long time. I'm concerned about her."

"She's been a little distraught," Colt said. "She truly believes that Dee might be dangerous and is concerned about you and your family."

"I gathered that," Hud said with a curse, then studied him for a long moment. "I get the feeling you agree with her."

"I think there is cause for concern." He hurried on, before Hud could argue differently, knowing he was in dangerous territory. "You never laid eyes on this woman before she showed up at your door. You can't even be sure she is who she says she is."

"Dana sent her a certified letter that she had to sign for at her current address. And I've seen her identification."

That surprised Colt. "Then you *were* suspicious."

Hud sighed. "I had to be after the allegations Hilde was making. But she checks out, and Dana is enjoying her visit. She thinks Hilde is jealous. I can see that you don't agree."

"I'm just saying, you might want to keep an eye on her, that's all."

His boss looked as if there was more he wanted to say. Or more he was hoping his deputy would. But Colt held his tongue. His friend at the crime lab had promised to run the prints as quickly as he could.

Whatever the outcome, he hadn't figured out what to do after that. Until then, there was little he *could* do.

"We finally got a positive identification on Rick Cameron," Hud said, and tossed the man's file across his desk to Colt.

He opened it, glanced at the latest entry and jerked his head up in surprise. "Richard Northland?" So he hadn't been using his real name at all?

Hud nodded. "And before you ask, Dee had no idea he was lying about his name."

Colt let out a laugh as he tossed the file back. "As your friend? Get Dee out of your house. As your deputy? I really should get to work."

HILDE WAS LOST in the memory of last night with Colt as she unlocked Needles and Pins. Dinner had been magical. The lovemaking had been beyond anything she'd ever experienced. She'd been lost in a dream state all morning.

That's why it took her a moment to realize what she was seeing.

The shop had been vandalized.

Bolts of fabric were now scattered over the floor. Displays had been toppled, and spools of thread littered the areas of the floor that weren't covered by fabric bolts.

She fumbled her phone from her purse, her heart pounding as she realized whoever had done this could still be in the shop. That was when she noticed the back door standing open. The vandal had left a large roll of yellow rickrack trailing out the back door like the equivalent of a bread trail through the shop.

"911. What is your emergency?" she heard an operator say.

"My shop has been vandalized," Hilde said.

"You're calling from Big Sky?"

"Yes. Needles and Pins."

"Is the vandal still there?"

"No. I don't believe so."

"Please wait outside until the marshal or one of his deputies arrive. Do you need to stay on the phone with me?"

"No. I just can't imagine who would—" That's when Hilde saw the scissors. Six of them. All stabbed into the top of her counter just inches from where she'd pretended to attack Dee to get the woman's fingerprints.

"You look tired," Dana said when Dee came down-stairs. "Did you sleep all right?"

"Like a baby." Once she got into bed again. Last night's exploits had left her exhausted. Clearly just what she'd needed since once she'd hit the sheets, she hadn't had the nightmare again.

Dana was busy with the kids as usual. "It might be just as well that I don't have anything planned for you today. Maybe a day just resting would do us all good."

Dee didn't know how the woman managed with four kids. She'd apparently just finished feeding the two oldest because she was only now clearing away their plates. She sent them off to the bathroom to wash up.

The two youngest were in some kind of contraptions that allowed them to roll around the kitchen. They'd gotten caught in a corner and one of them was holler-ing his head off.

Dana saved him, kneeling down to cajole him be-fore she asked, "I made Mary and Hank pancakes, Dee. Would you like some?"

The kitchen smelled of pancakes and maple syrup. Dee heard her stomach growl. She was starved, also probably because of all the exercise she'd gotten last night. She'd been careful to stay away from any street-lights, and she was sure no one had seen her leaving and returning to the ranch.

"I'd love pancakes, but let me make them," Dee of-fered, knowing Dana wouldn't take her up on it.

"It's no trouble. Anyway, you're my guest."

Dee could hear something in Dana's voice, though. Her hostess was tiring of her guest. Probably all the drama. Dana would be glad when Dee left.

Well, there was nothing she could do about that, because the drama was far from over. Forced to move up her plan, she said, "I'm thinking I've stayed too long."

Dana turned from the stove. "No. I don't want you to feel that way at all. I'm just sorry. I really wanted you to have a good time."

"I *am* having a good time." Dee went over and gave Dana a hug. "But I need to get back home and look for a job. I can't be off work for too long." Sometimes she couldn't believe how easy lying came to her. She was more amazed by people who couldn't tell a lie. Maybe it was a talent you were born with.

Or maybe you had to learn it at your daddy's knee, she thought bitterly.

"I checked this morning about a flight," she said with equal effortlessness. "I'm booked for Saturday on a nonstop flight to LaGuardia." She knew Dana and Hud wouldn't check to see if it was true or not. But Colt might.

Dana didn't try to get her to change her mind. *Yep, it's time.* She just said, "Well, I hate to see you cut your trip short, but you know best."

"This isn't my only trip to Cardwell Ranch," Dee said.

"Well, I insist on paying for your flight." Dana held up her hand even though Dee hadn't protested. "No arguments. I want this trip to be my treat."

"That is so sweet of you. I'm going to pay you back, though, and then some." By booking the nonstop flight that was available only on Saturday, she had bought herself a little more time. It wasn't perfect timing, but she'd have to make it work, especially after finding her toothbrush and makeup missing. She'd already put the wheels in motion. *Hang on,* she thought, because she knew what was about to hit the fan.

Dana looked visibly relaxed now that she knew her guest was leaving. Dee hated Hilde at that moment. The woman had been a thorn in her side from the beginning. If she had just backed off… But it was too late for regrets, she thought, and checked her watch.

Any minute poor Hilde would be crying on the marshal's shoulder and no doubt blaming her.

MARSHAL HUD SAVAGE stopped in the doorway of Needles and Pins and demanded, "What are you doing?"

"I'm cleaning up my shop," Hilde said, as she placed another bolt of fabric back where it went. She was thankful that most of the fabrics hadn't gotten soiled or ruined. Dee could have torn up the place much worse. Hilde knew she should be thankful for that.

She'd started cleaning up the moment she'd realized who'd done this. At that same moment, she'd known there was no reason to wait for the marshal. Hud wasn't going to believe Dee had done this. And the only way to try to change his mind would be to show him the scissors and explain why they were a message from Dee.

Hilde couldn't do that without telling what she'd done to get Dee's fingerprints and Colt's involvement. She wasn't about to drag him into this any more than he already was.

"You shouldn't have touched anything until I got here," Hud said behind her. "Hilde—"

She stopped working to look at him. Fueled by anger, she'd accomplished a lot in a short time. "The person broke in through the back. I haven't touched anything back there."

He looked toward the back of the shop, where she had a small kitchen she and her staff used as a break and storage room. She'd found a chair moved over against the wall under the open window. There appeared to be marks on the window frame where someone had pried it open.

When she'd stepped outside in the alley, she'd discovered the large trash container pulled over under the window.

Hud went back in the break room, then outside. "Is anything missing?" he asked when he came back in.

"I don't believe so. I don't leave money down here. I think it was just a malicious act of vandalism."

"Looks like it might have been kids, then," Hud said.

Hilde had stopped to look at him, after restoring almost all of the bolts of fabric to their correct places. She saw him staring at the countertop where the half-dozen new scissors had been stuck in the wood.

"Kids resort to this sort of thing just for something to do, I guess," he said.

"It wasn't kids." She crossed her arms because she was trembling and she didn't want him to see it. She thought that if she kept calm and didn't get upset or cry, he might believe her.

"Don't tell me Dee did this." He looked as resolute as she felt.

"Okay, I won't. You don't want to hear the truth, fine. Kids did it."

"Hilde," Hud said in that tone she was getting used

to. "Dee went to bed last night before we did. If she had driven into town, I would have known it."

"Maybe she walked."

"It's a couple of miles. She can barely walk around the yard without twisting an ankle. You think she climbed up into that window back there?" He was shaking his head. "I'm sorry this happened. I'll file a report and you can turn it over to your insurance. I'm glad nothing was destroyed."

She laughed at that. Dee had destroyed so much—the shop was the least of it.

"Are you going to be okay?"

The concern and kindness she heard in his tone was her undoing. The tears broke loose as if they had been walled up, waiting for the least bit of provocation to burst out.

He patted her shoulder. "Take the rest of the day off. Go home. Get some rest."

As if rest would make her world right again.

FORTUNATELY, THE REST of the day was busy at the shop. All the women who'd come in to sign up for quilting classes buoyed Hilde's spirits.

Dana called midmorning. "Just wanted to say hi."

Hilde figured she'd heard about the vandalism from Hud. He must not have told her about the allegations against her cousin.

"Fourteen women have signed up for the quilting classes so far," she told her silent partner in the shop.

"Oh, that's great. You must be excited to get them started."

"I am. It's going to be a good summer." Hilde said the last like a mantra, praying it was true.

"Dee's leaving Saturday," Dana said.

The words should have made her heart soar, but she heard sadness in her friend's voice. "I'm sorry her visit didn't go like you had hoped."

The bell over the door jangled as another customer came in.

Dana must have heard it. "You're busy. I'll let you go. I just wanted you to know I was thinking about you."

"Thank you for calling." It was the best she could do before Dana hung up.

The rest of the day slipped by. Hilde had moments when she would forget about the break-in. She knew she would have to replace the top of the counter. The scissor holes were a gut-wrenching reminder each time she saw them that it wasn't over with Dee.

Colt must have called when she was helping a customer by carrying her fabric purchases out to her car. He'd left a message that he hoped he could see her tonight.

She texted back that she was looking forward to it.

And suddenly it was time to close up shop. She gathered her things, trying hard not to look at the top of the counter. Thinking about Dee only made her blood boil.

A gust of wind caught the door as she started to lock up. She hadn't realized the wind had come up or that a storm was blowing in.

As she turned, she saw that her SUV parked across the street was sitting at a funny angle. Then she noticed the right back tire. Flat.

All she'd been thinking about the past few minutes

was going home, taking a nice hot bath and getting ready for when Colt got back from West Yellowstone.

After finding her store vandalized first thing in the morning, she wasn't going to let a flat tire ruin her mood now, she thought. For a moment, she considered changing the tire herself, but she wasn't dressed for it, and her house was only a short walk from the shop.

As she started down the street, she saw that the storm was closer than she'd thought. Dark clouds rolled in, dimming the remainder of the day's light. She'd be lucky to get home before it started to rain, and in April the rain could easily turn to snow.

Hilde laughed, surprised that even the storm didn't bother her. She was seeing Colt again tonight and she couldn't wait. The only real dark cloud right now was Dee Anna Justice, and apparently there wasn't a darned thing she could do about her.

When she looked up and saw Dee coming down the dark street toward her, she feared she'd conjured her. Because of the upcoming storm and the time of the year, the streets were deserted—something she hadn't noticed until that moment.

Stopping, she considered what to do. Dee had realized that she had her fingerprints and DNA. That was probably why she'd torn up the shop. Did that mean she'd realized whatever she'd been up to was about to come to a screeching halt? Or would the prints only prove that the woman really was Dee Anna Justice, a psychopath who would be able to keep fooling Dana unless Hilde and Colt could prove otherwise?

More to the immediate point, what was she doing here now? Hilde considered whether she should make a run for it. She didn't have that many options. Calling the marshal's office for help would be a waste of time.

"You don't have to look so scared," Dee called to her. "I came to give you some news that I think will make you happy."

Hilde let the woman get within a few feet of her. "That's close enough. What is it?"

"You win."

"You're the one who made it into a competition."

Dee chuckled as she took another step closer. "I've known women like you my whole life. Everything comes so easy to you. You've never had to fight for anything. You wouldn't have lasted two seconds in my world."

"I'm sorry you had a rough life, Dee, if that is really your name. But that doesn't give you the right to take someone else's—literally."

"You're right," Dee said, not even bothering to deny anything. "I'm leaving. I just wanted you to know. That, and I'm sorry. I don't expect you to understand. I don't even understand why I'm like I am sometimes." She put her head down, actually sounding as if she meant it.

Hilde wondered what kind of life this woman really *had* lived through. Dee was right that her own had been cushy. As much as she hated it, she felt some sympathy for the woman. "You should try to get some help."

Dee slowly raised her head. It took Hilde an instant to realize Dee had stepped closer during all this. When she met her gaze, Hilde saw that something had changed in her eyes. It was an instant too long.

Before Hilde could react, Dee grabbed her right hand and raked Hilde's nails down her own left cheek.

Hilde let out a cry of shock and jerked her hand back.

Dee was smiling as she touched the four angry scratches down her face. Laughing at Hilde's reaction, she reached down and picked up a chunk of broken sidewalk at the edge of the street.

Hilde took a step back as Dee said, "You think I need help? Maybe I *should* see someone." She hit herself in the face with the piece of concrete and for a moment, Hilde thought Dee would buckle under the savage blow. But she straightened, dropped the chunk of sidewalk and, in the next instant, began to tear at her clothes.

"What are you doing?" Hilde cried. "Have you lost your mind?"

"Isn't this what you wish you were able to do to me?" Dee asked, smiling again. Her left eye was already swelling shut from where she'd hit herself. There was blood at the corner of her mouth and her lip was split and bleeding. The scratches down the left side of her face were bleeding now as well.

"No, I would never—" The rest of Hilde's words died on her lips as she realized exactly what Dee *was* doing. "No one will believe I did that to you!"

"Won't they?" Dee asked with a smirk. "Wanna bet?" With that she turned and ran screaming down the street.

Chapter Eleven

Hilde rushed back to Needles and Pins, fumbled the key in the lock and, once inside, relocked the door behind her. She was in shock, never having witnessed anything like that in her life.

Her hands shook as she took out her cell phone. She tried to call Colt but only got his voice mail. She left a message that it was urgent she talk to him. Only after she hung up did she remember he had to go back to West Yellowstone today.

She'd barely hung up when she saw Marshal Hud Savage pull up in his patrol pickup in front of the shop. Past him, across the street, she spotted her SUV with the flat tire. She hadn't had a flat in years. Why hadn't she realized it was a trap?

Because that wasn't how her mind worked. She'd never had to read evil into everything—until Dee arrived in town.

Hilde felt like a fool. She'd played right into the woman's hands, not once, but time and again. The more she protested, the worse it got. She knew that even if she hadn't started to walk home, Dee would have found an opportunity to make this happen.

Lightning cut a zigzagged line across the sky behind

Hud as he headed for her front door. Thunder followed on its heels. Large drops of rain pelted the sidewalk as she put her cell phone back in her purse and hurried to unlock the shop door. "Hud, I—"

"I need you to come with me down to the station," he said, his voice hard as the sidewalk Dee had hit herself with.

"I didn't do any of that to her," Hilde cried. "Hud, you have to believe me."

He grabbed her right hand, holding it up. "Hilde, her skin is still under your fingernails."

"Hud, I know this sounds crazy, but that's the problem. Dee, or whatever her name is, *is* crazy. She's insane. She did all of that to herself."

He shook his head looking as sad as she had ever seen him. "Are you telling me you didn't attack her previously with a pair of scissors right here in your shop?"

Of course Dee would have told him about that, too. "No. I mean, yes, but—"

He began to read her rights to her. "Let's go," he said when he finished.

"You're really arresting me?" She couldn't believe any of this was happening. "You know me, Hud—"

"I thought I did. Dee Anna is pressing assault charges against you. Hilde, what is going on with you?"

She swallowed and shook her head. Even if she told him about the scissors incident, it wouldn't help her. Nor help Colt. She just had to put her faith in Colt to find out the truth about the woman—and soon.

COLT TRIED TO reach Hilde the moment he got her message. Her phone went straight to voice mail. He called the shop, just in case she was working late. She did that a lot, especially since she'd recently taken over the space next to Needles and Pins and expanded the business.

She was buying a line of sewing machines and would be starting quilting lessons, now that she had the room. He loved her work ethic. Loved a lot of things about her, he thought, reminded of last night.

With growing concern when she didn't answer at the shop, he realized he didn't know whom else to call. Not that long ago, he could have called Dana. She would have known where Hilde was. Dana and Hilde had been that close.

But not now. Thanks to Dee.

He was holding his phone, trying to decide what to do, when it rang. It was one of the dispatchers, Annie Wagner, a cute twentysomething redhead who was dating a Bozeman police officer he knew.

"I thought you'd want to know," Annie said in a hushed voice. "Hilde has been arrested."

"What?" His mind whirled. Hilde?

"Dee Anna Justice came screaming into the office thirty minutes ago saying Hilde had attacked her."

Colt groaned. He'd understood Hilde's thinking with the scissors, but—

"Dee was a mess. She looked like she'd gotten into a cat fight. Black eye, scratched up, bleeding."

He couldn't imagine Hilde doing that to anyone even if she was provoked. But if she was defending herself— "Where is Hilde now?"

"Hud has her in his office. I just put through a call from Dee Anna Justice. Do you want me to call you if anything changes?"

"Thanks, Annie. I appreciate it. I'm on my way back from West Yellowstone. I should be there within the hour."

What had happened? He couldn't even imagine.

He'd told himself that Hud would see through Dee soon. Or Dee would give up once she realized Hud loved Dana and would never fall for her. He'd told himself that as long as Hilde stayed away from the ranch and Dee, this wouldn't escalate.

He'd been wrong. He also realized that until that moment, he hadn't really thought Dee had tried to kill Hilde. The scare at the falls had been just that. The incident under the raft? He thought Dee had probably pulled the same thing. Held Hilde under the raft then tried to save her, only this time Hilde had fought her off.

Now he was angry with himself for not truly believing what Hilde had known in her heart. Dee was capable of horrendous things. Even murder. Maybe she'd drugged Rick. What had she done to get Hilde arrested? Tried to kill her only to have Hilde fight back?

His heart was pounding as he switched on his lights and siren and raced toward Big Sky.

HILDE KNEW SHE was lucky that Hud hadn't brought her into jail in handcuffs. She figured that might be Dana's doing. Dana would go to bat for her even if she believed that her once best friend had attacked her cousin.

It still amazed her that anyone would believe Dee. But look at the extremes the woman would go to. She *was* insane. How else could Hilde explain it? Insane and desperate. This was a ploy to keep Hilde from getting her fingerprints run. Which had to mean that Dee really wasn't Dee Anna Justice—just as the now deceased Rick had insinuated.

But none of that helped Hilde right now, she thought, as she looked across the marshal's big desk. He was on the phone and had been for several minutes. From his tone of voice, she suspected it had been Dana who'd called, but Hilde now thought that Dana had put Dee on the line.

"I do understand," Hud was saying. "But I'd prefer that you came down here and we discussed this before you made any—" He listened for a moment, his gaze going to Hilde, before he said, "If you're sure. I would strongly advise you against this." More listening, then he said, "Fine," and hung up.

Hilde hadn't realized that she'd been holding her breath toward the end of his conversation until she let it out as he hung up.

Hud sat for a moment before he turned to her. "Dee is dropping the charges. I can still hold you, if I want to, and I'm certainly considering it."

She could tell that Dana had fought for her. Why else would Dee have dropped the charges? She felt tears sting her eyes. She knew better than to argue that she hadn't done anything to Dee. She'd already tried the truth and that had gotten her arrested, so she waited.

"Dee is filing a temporary restraining order that is good for twenty days. I assume you know what that is," he said.

A restraining order? It was all she could do not to scream. "It means I can't go near her." Which meant she couldn't go near the ranch or Dana. Her tears now were of frustration. Dee kept maneuvering her into impossible situations where Hilde always came out look-ing like the villain.

"That's going to be hard to do in Big Sky. Hilde," he said with a sigh. "Think about taking a vacation. Go see your mother in Chicago. Or go lay on a beach for a couple of weeks. Get out of here."

"For twenty days?" Wouldn't Dee love that. "Or maybe she'll make it a permanent restraining order, since she doesn't seem to be leaving, does she?"

"Hilde, I'm trying to help. I'd think you'd want to get out of here for a while."

"You don't know how tempting that is, Hud." She felt as beat-up as Dee was. She'd lost control of her life. She'd certainly lost her friends, her shop had been van-dalized and she was losing faith that she would ever be able to fix any of this before things got worse.

"Dana is worried about you," he said, and she heard some of that old caring in his voice.

"And I'm worried about her. I wish I *could* leave, but I can't, Hud. I can't leave Dana knowing what's living in your house right now. I'm sorry," she said when she saw his expression harden. "So can I go now?"

He nodded. "Hilde? Stay away from Dee."

"Believe me, I'm doing my best. For the record, do you want to actually hear the truth?" She didn't wait for him to answer. "I came out of the shop after lock-ing up to find I had a flat tire. I should have suspected something then, but I've never been a suspicious person. I started to walk home, no big deal, that's when I saw Dee. She called to me, said she had some news. When she got close, she told me she was leaving. She said she was sorry for what she'd done to me."

Hilde stopped for a moment, smiled and said, "You know I actually believed her. She is that good. And then she grabbed my hand, raked my fingernails down her face. I was so shocked I couldn't move. I jerked my hand back. That's when she picked up a chunk of broken sidewalk from the side of the street and hit herself in the face. I know," she said, seeing his disbelieving expression. "I had the same reaction. Right after that was when she began to rip her clothing. She said no one would believe me. So far, she's been dead-on, hasn't she?"

With that she turned and walked out, leaving Hud frowning after her.

ONLY A FEW miles out of Big Sky, Colt got the call that Dee was refusing to press charges, deciding to take out a temporary restraining order instead. He swore, anxious to get to Hilde and find out what had happened.

He found her at her house. She hadn't been home long when she opened the door. He saw that she had a stunned look on her face. Stunned and devastated. It was heartbreaking.

Without a word, he took her in his arms. She was trembling. He took her over to the couch, then went to her liquor cabinet and found some bourbon. He poured her a couple fingers' worth.

"Drink this," he said.

"Aren't you afraid what I might do liquored up?" she asked sarcastically.

"Terrified," he said and stood over her until she'd downed every drop. "You want to talk about it?" he asked, taking the empty glass from her and joining her on the couch.

She let out a laugh. "*I* hardly believe what happened. Why would I expect anyone else to?"

"I believe you. I believe everything you've told me."

Tears welled in her brown eyes. He drew her to him and kissed her, holding her tightly. "I'm sorry you had to go through this alone."

She nodded and wiped hastily at the tears as she drew back to look at him. "You're my only hope right now. We have to find out whatever we can about this woman." And then she told him everything, from finding the shop vandalized to what led up to her being nearly arrested.

When she finished, he said, "We shouldn't be surprised."

"Surprised? I'm still in shock. To do something like that to yourself..."

"You knew Dee was sick."

Hilde nodded. "What will she do next? That's what worries me."

Colt didn't want to say it, but that worried him, too. "Maybe Hud has the right idea. Isn't there somewhere—"

"I'm not leaving. Dee told me that I've never had to fight for anything. Well, I'm fighting now. I'm bringing her down. One way or another."

"Hilde—"

"She has to be stopped."

"I agree. But we have to be careful. She's dangerous." He felt his phone vibrate, checked it and saw that his boss had sent him a text. "Hud wants to see me ASAP." Not good. "I don't want to leave you here alone."

"I'll be fine. Dee won this round. She won't do anything for a while, and I'm not going to give her another chance to use me like she did today."

He heard the courage as well as the determination in her voice. Hilde was strong and, no matter what Dee had told her, she *was* a fighter.

"Would you mind if I came by later?"

Her kiss answered that question quite nicely.

HUD WAS WAITING when Colt arrived. He motioned him into his office. "What the hell do you think you're doing?" he said the moment Colt closed the door and sat down.

"I beg your pardon?" He had a pretty good idea what the problem was, but he wasn't about to hand him the rope to hang him.

"Tell me about the unauthorized request to run fingerprints you sent to the crime lab," the marshal said.

That's what Colt figured. Someone had caught his friend. He hated that he'd gotten the man into trouble. Sticking out his own neck was one thing. Sticking out someone else's was a whole other story.

"They're the woman's now staying at your house, the one you call Dee Anna Justice," he said.

Hud swore and slammed a hand down on his desk as he sat forward. "What the hell were you thinking sending an unauthorized request to the crime lab?"

"I was trying to protect you and your family."

"That isn't going to wash and you know it. Well, let me give you the news. There are no prints on file."

Hud let that sink in. "That's right. Dee has no record. Satisfied?"

So she'd never been arrested. That didn't surprise him given what he'd seen of her maneuvers so far.

"This is about Hilde, isn't it?" Hud demanded. "You did this for her. This is so you can get closer to her."

Colt got to his feet. "If that's what you think—"

"You're suspended."

This, too, didn't come as a surprise. He met Hud's gaze. "If you really think I would use law enforcement resources to try to get a woman in bed, then I think you should fire me."

"Damn it, Colt, you're a fine deputy marshal and I don't want to lose you. Two weeks without pay. Get out of here."

He left Hud's office, knowing there was nothing he could say. He'd taken a risk. It had cost him. Worse, it had only made Dee look more innocent.

"Colt," Annie whispered, as he started for the door out of the station. He could tell that she'd probably heard everything. The department was small, the walls thin. She motioned him over and secretly slipped him a folded sheet of paper. "I think you'll want to see this."

They both heard Hud come out of his office. Colt mouthed *Thank you* and quickly left. It wasn't until he reached home that he finally unfolded the sheet and saw what was written on it.

He went straight to his computer. It didn't take long before he found what he was looking for—and then some.

Chapter Twelve

Hilde knew things hadn't gone well at the marshal's office the moment she opened the door and saw Colt's face.

"What happened?" she asked, as she let him in.

"Nothing to worry about."

"He found out that you sent Dee's fingerprints to the crime lab."

"I knew there was a chance that might happen."

"Tell me he didn't fire you," she cried.

"He didn't. Suspended for two weeks. As it turns out, the suspension couldn't come at a better time. I've got some news."

They moved into the kitchen, where Hilde got him a beer and poured a glass of wine for herself. She had a feeling she was going to need it. "I hate getting you into trouble."

"You didn't. I'm in this just as deep as you are," he said, and kissed her as he took the cold bottle of beer she offered him. He took a sip. She watched him, desire making her legs weak as water.

She dropped into a chair in front of the fireplace, curling her legs under her and taking a drink of her wine. She'd built a small fire since he'd said he would be back. She'd tried not to count the minutes.

Colt didn't sit but stood in front of the fire. She could tell he was worked up, too antsy to sit.

"You have news?" she asked, afraid what he was about to tell her.

"Rick Cameron's real name was Richard Northland. Cameron was apparently one of a number of aliases he has used. He was a small-time con artist, been arrested a couple of times, but nothing that got him more than a little jail time. The person he cheated tended to drop the charges."

Hilde felt her eyes widen. "So he and Dee had a lot in common."

"I'm sure Dee was shocked by the news when Hud told her."

Hilde let out a humorless laugh. "I'm sure she was."

"There's more. Her fingerprints weren't on file. But when I did some digging online, I found a story about Richard and his sister, Camilla Northland."

"His *sister?*"

Colt nodded. "The two of them were the only survivors of a fire at their home in Tuttle, Oklahoma. Both parents were killed. Apparently there was some suspicion that one or both might have purposely started the fire. Richard was fourteen at the time, Camilla sixteen."

"Are you saying what I think you are?" Hilde asked.

"I'm trying hard not to jump to any conclusions. All we know for sure is that the man lying in the morgue is Richard Northland from Tuttle, Oklahoma. I'll know more once I get there."

"Get there?"

"I'm flying to Oklahoma tomorrow on the first flight out."

Hilde got up from her chair and moved to the fire as a sudden chill skittered across her skin like spider legs. "You think there's a possibility that Dee is his sister?"

"A possibility based on nothing more than a feeling that the two of them knew each other longer than Dee said."

She recalled how Rick had turned around when the naked Dee had gotten out of the lake. "Dana thought Rick was Dee's boyfriend."

"Probably because that's what she told her. I haven't been able to find out much of anything about Camilla because she dropped off radar right after the fire. According to a newspaper account, the two were going to live with an aunt since their parents were the only family they had."

"She dropped off the radar because she's not using her real name?"

"That would be my guess. While I'm gone I want you to stay clear of Dee."

"If she finds out where you've gone…"

"She won't. I'll tell someone at the station that I'm going to Denver to see my brother. I'm sure by now they all know I've been suspended."

"Colt," she said, touching his strong shoulder. "I don't want to see you lose your job."

"I won't. I think whatever I find out in Oklahoma will change things drastically."

Hilde couldn't help being nervous. "Be careful. I'm just afraid what Dee might do if she thinks you're onto her. So far it's just me she's after."

"Yeah, that's what worries me. Look what happened to Rick," Colt said.

Hilde shivered and he took her in his arms. "I just don't want her moving up her plan, whatever it is."

"I'm more worried about you. I wish you were going with me."

"If we both went, it would look even more suspicious. Anyway, she's accomplished what she set out to do. Dana and I are hardly speaking."

"I hate seeing you like this," he said, and kissed her. "It's going to be all right. I know you're worried about Dana. But we're going to get this resolved."

She nodded. "Hopefully before something horrible happens."

"Hilde, I don't think Dee is through with you, so be careful."

"I will."

"Promise?"

She smiled and leaned up to kiss him. "I'll be careful."

"I'll call you from Oklahoma as soon as I know something. I won't be gone any longer than I have to. I'm going home to pack, but first..." He swung her up in his arms. "I don't want you to forget about me while I'm gone."

"Like that could happen," she said with a laugh, as he carried her into the bedroom.

COLT TRIED TO get on standby, but the earliest flight he could get on was that afternoon. He hated leaving Hilde. Last night he'd managed to talk her into letting Ronnie open the shop and man it until he got back. It had taken some talking, though. Hilde was one determined woman.

He tried not to speculate on what Dee might do. When he'd called Annie at the office, he'd told her he was flying to Denver to visit his brother. Of course, she knew he'd been suspended.

"Mrs. Savage was in earlier," Annie told him in a hushed whisper. "She and the boss had a row over your suspension. Seems her cousin has booked a flight to New York City for Saturday."

That had been news. Saturday was only two days away. If Dee was telling the truth. "I suppose there is no way to find out if she really did book that flight," he said to Annie.

She chuckled. "I'll see what I can do."

After he hung up, he wondered if this meant Dee was giving up. Maybe she'd realized that Hilde had her fingerprints and DNA, so it wouldn't be long before they knew who she really was. *Best to leave town before that happened, huh, Dee?*

His plane landed in Salt Lake City with a short layover before he flew into Oklahoma City, where he rented a car. It was too late to drive to Tuttle, so he got a motel. When he called Hilde, she sounded fine, anxious, but staying in the house. He breathed a sigh of relief.

"Try to get some sleep," he told her. "I won't know anything until tomorrow at the soonest." He didn't sleep well at all and early the next morning set off for Tuttle.

The town had once been a tiny suburb. Now the buildings along the former main street were boarded up. It was one of many small, dying towns across the country.

Colt stopped at the combination grocery and gas station and wandered inside. A fan whirred in the window near the counter behind an elderly woman who sat thumbing through a movie magazine.

"Can you believe all the divorces they have out in Hollywood?" She looked up at him over her glasses as if actually expecting an answer.

"No, I can't."

She closed the magazine, studying him. "You aren't from around here."

He shook his head. "But I'm looking for someone *from* around here."

Her eyes widened a little. "I figured you were just lost. Who are you looking for? I know most everyone since I was born and raised right here."

That had been his hope. "Maybe you know them, then. Richard and Camilla Northland?

The woman's expression soured in a heartbeat. She leaned back as if trying to distance herself from his words. "Well, you won't find them around here."

"Actually, I'm looking for their aunt, the one who raised them after their parents died."

"Didn't die. Were murdered." She shook her head. "What do you want with Thelma?"

"I have some news about her nephew."

"There isn't any news she'd want to hear except that he's six feet under," the woman snapped.

"Then I guess I have some good news for her."

HILDE TRIED NOT to go down to the shop the next day, but Ronnie called to say there was a problem with the new sewing machine invoice and the deliveryman wasn't sure what she wanted him to do.

"I'll be right there." She was thankful for the call. Sitting around waiting to hear from Colt was making her all the more anxious. She was also thankful that the sewing machines hadn't arrived before Dee vandalized the shop.

Once at the shop after taking care of the problem, Hilde showed Ronnie some of the ideas she had for quilting classes, and they began to work on a wall hanging for the sewing room.

Hilde loved the way the shop was coming together. She'd long dreamed of a place where anyone who wanted to learn to quilt could come and sew with others of like mind. Quilting was a restful and yet creative hobby at any age. She had great plans for the future and was so excited about them that she'd almost picked up the phone and called Dana to tell her.

Dana still had money invested in Needles and Pins. Hilde realized that might change now. She should consider buying her out if their friendship went any further south. The thought made her sad. If only they could prove that Dee wasn't her cousin.

She was mentally kicking herself for not thinking to take Dana's toothbrush as well as Dee's, when the bell over the door jangled and she turned to see Dana walk into the shop.

Hilde felt her face light up—until she saw Dana's expression. Her stomach fell with the memory of what had happened yesterday. Dana must be horrified. But how could her once best friend not realize that Hilde could never beat up anyone?

She felt a spark of anger, which she quickly tamped down as Dana stepped into the shop. Letting her temper flare was a surefire way to make herself look more guilty.

"Could we talk alone?" Dana asked quietly.

"Ronnie, would you mind watching the counter for a few minutes?" Hilde called. Ronnie said she'd be happy to. Hilde led Dana into the break room and closed the door. She didn't want Ronnie hearing this. But the news was probably all over town anyway. The shop had been unusually slow today.

"I don't know what to say to you," Dana said.

Hilde stepped to the coffeepot, fingers trembling as she took two clean glass cups and filled each with coffee. She handed one to Dana, then sat down, ready for a lecture.

Dana seemed to hesitate before she sat down. Hilde didn't help her by denying anything. Instead she waited, relieved when Dana finally took a drink of the coffee and seemed to calm down some.

"How long have we known each other?" Hilde asked.

Dana looked up from her cup in surprise. "Since you came to town about…six years ago. But you know that."

"So for six years we've been close friends. Some might even have said best friends."

Dana's eyes suddenly shone with tears.

"Would you have said you knew me well?" She didn't wait for an answer. "Remember that spider in my kitchen that time? I couldn't squish it. You had to do it."

"You can't compare killing a spider to—"

"Dana, what if Dee wasn't your cousin?"

"That's ridiculous because she *is* my cousin."

Hilde wasn't going to argue that. Not right now anyway. "What if she was just some stranger who ended up on your doorstep and things began happening and the next thing you knew you and I were…" She couldn't bring herself to say where they were. "Would you take a stranger's word over mine?"

Dana put down her cup. "She said you would say you didn't attack her."

Hilde sighed and put down her own cup. "That you came here today makes me believe that there is some doubt in your mind. I hope that's true, because it might save your life."

"It's talk like that, Hilde, that makes me think you've lost your mind," Dana said, getting to her feet. "Why would Dee want to hurt me?"

"So she could have Hud."

Dana shook her head. "Hud loves *me*."

"But if you were gone…"

Dana reached into her jeans pocket and took out a piece of paper. Hilde recognized it as a sheet from the notepad Dana kept by the phone. "I called around. This is the name of a doctor everyone said was very good." When Hilde didn't reach for the note, Dana laid it on the table. "I think you need help, Hilde." Her voice broke with emotion.

"She doesn't just want you out of the way, Dana. Your children will have to go, too."

Dana's gaze came up to meet hers.

Hilde saw fear. "Trust me. Trust the friendship we had. You're in trouble. So are your babies."

A tear trailed down Dana's cheek. She brushed at it.

"I have to go." She hurried out, leaving Hilde alone in the break room.

The moment she heard the bell jangle, Hilde got up, took a plastic bag from the drawer and carefully bagged Dana's coffee cup.

"What are you doing?"

She turned in surprise to find Dana standing in the doorway. She must have started to leave, but then changed her mind.

"I asked you what you were doing."

Hilde knew there was no reason to lie even if she could have thought of one Dana might believe. "I need your DNA to check it against Dee's."

The shocked look on Dana's face said it all. That and what she said before turning and really leaving this time: "Oh, Hilde."

COLT DROVE OUT of Tuttle, took the third right and pulled down a narrow two-track toward a stand of live oak. He hadn't been in the South in years. Oklahoma wasn't considered the South to people from Georgia or Alabama, but anywhere that cotton grew along the road was the South to him.

He followed the directions the woman at the grocery and gas station had given him until the road played out, ending in front of a weathered, stooped old house that was much like the elderly woman who came out on the porch.

He parked and climbed out. Thelma Peters was Richard and Camilla Northland's aunt on their mother's side of the family, PJ Harris had told him.

"Everyone's called me PJ since I was a girl," the elderly woman at the store had told him. "Not because it has anything to do with my name, which by the way is Charlotte Elizabeth. No, I got PJ because that's what I was usually wearing when I would come down here, to this very store, in the morning so my father could make me breakfast. My mother had died when I was a baby, you see. He'd pour me a bowl of cereal, ask me if I wanted berries. I always said no, then he'd pour on some thick cream." Her eyes had lit at the memory. "I can still taste that cream. Can't buy anything like it anymore."

He'd finally managed to turn her back to Richard and Camilla's aunt.

"Thelma Peters. She's an old maid. I can see where having those two in her house turned her against ever having any of her own children." PJ had studied him again then. "Don't be surprised if she comes out on her porch with a shotgun. Don't take it personally. Just make sure she knows you aren't that no-count nephew of hers. I'd hate to see you get shot."

"I'll keep that in mind," he'd promised.

"I'm here with some good news," Colt called out now to the elderly old maid holding the shotgun.

"If you're preaching the Gospel, I've already found the Lord. You wasted your gas coming out here," she called back.

"I'm a deputy marshal from Montana," he called to her. A slight exaggeration at the moment. He saw the change in her as if she was bracing herself for whatever bad news he was bringing. "Your nephew Richard has been killed."

Thelma Peters nodded, then took a step back and sat down hard in an old wooden chair on her porch.

The barrel end of the shotgun banged against the worn wood flooring at her feet, but she held on to the gun as she motioned him to come closer.

Colt walked up to the house, shielding his eyes against the sun. The yard was a dust bowl. The weeds that had survived were baked dead. "I'm sorry to bring you the news."

She looked up then and, from rheumy but intelligent blue eyes, considered him for a long moment. "You certainly came a long way to give it to me."

"I need to ask you about Camilla."

Thelma let out a cough of a laugh. "You cross her path, too? Best say your prayers."

"I don't know if I've crossed her path or not. Do you happen to have a picture of her?"

The woman looked at him as if he was crazy. "Not one I keep out, I can tell you that."

"I sure would appreciate it if you could find one for me. I'm worried about a family in Montana that this woman has moved in with."

She grunted and pushed herself to her feet, using the shotgun like a crutch. "Better step inside. This could take a while."

When Dana came back from town, she was clearly upset.

"You didn't go see Hilde," Dee said, wanting to wring her neck. She'd begged her to stay away from her former friend. "Dana, what were you thinking?"

Hud, who'd come home to watch the kids while she ran to the store, seconded Dee's concern.

"I had to see her," Dana cried, then shook her head.

Dee had been so excited when Dana had told her that Hud was coming home to help her watch the children. She knew that neither of them wanted to leave the little darlings with her. She'd made it clear she knew nothing about kids, especially babies.

But all the time Hud had been home, he'd been so involved with the children that he wasn't even aware Dee was in the room.

"I hope you didn't listen to Hilde's crazy talk," Dee said, worried that that was exactly what Dana had done. She'd felt Dana pulling away from her. Worse, Hud was doing the same thing, she feared.

If only Hilde had just drowned that day under the raft.

Dee touched her sore black eye. "You're just lucky you didn't end up like me."

Dana glanced at her, wincing at the sight. Dee had to admit she looked like she'd been run over by a truck. But she'd wanted to make a statement and she had. Dana had been so thankful when she'd dropped the charges against Hilde. Even Hud had seemed relieved when he'd come home that night.

"It's worse than I thought," Dana said and looked at Hud. "I sat down and had a cup of coffee with her at the shop…"

Dee gritted her teeth in anger. How could Dana do that after seeing what Hilde had done to her cousin?

"She seemed calm, even rational…" Dana glanced at Dee then back at Hud.

Dee felt her heart begin to race. Hilde had gotten to Dana. She'd started believing her.

"Then I got ready to leave, made it as far as the door,

thought of something and went back." She stopped and took a breath. "Hud, she was bagging my coffee cup."

Dee let out a silent curse that was like a roar in her ears.

"I demanded to know what she was doing," Dana continued now in tears. "She told me she was going to check my DNA against Dee's. I'm sorry, Dee," Dana said, turning to her again. "I'm so sorry."

"Don't be. Clearly Hilde has had some sort of psychotic episode. How can she think I'm not your cousin? We look so much alike."

Dana nodded, still obviously upset.

"I'd ask who she thought she was going to get to run the tests, but I'm sure Colt is helping her," Hud said. "I can't imagine what he's thinking."

"I thought you said he went to Denver to see his brother?" Dee asked.

"That's what I heard, but I have my doubts. I can't see him leaving Hilde alone now. He must be as worried about her as we are."

THELMA PETERS'S HOUSE was small and cramped. She left him in a threadbare chair in the living room and disappeared into a room at the back. Periodically he would hear a bump or bang.

He looked around, noticing a picture of Jesus on one wall and a cross on another. A Bible lay open on the table next to his chair. He picked it up, curious what part she'd been reading. She had a passage underlined—Acts 3:19. *Repent therefore, and turn again, that your sins may be blotted out.*

"Here is the only one I could find." Thelma came

back into the room with a snapshot clutched in her fingers. "I haven't seen Camilla in years, so I don't know what she looks like now. But this is what she looked like at sixteen."

Chapter Thirteen

Colt looked down at the photo. His heart sank. The photo was of two people, a young man and a girl with long dark hair. The young man was the same man still at the morgue in Montana—Rick Cameron, aka Richard Northland.

The girl—was definitely not Dee.

He told himself it had been a long shot, but now realized how much he'd been counting on Dee being Camilla Northland. Maybe Rick really was her boyfriend. Maybe she didn't even kill him.

"This isn't the woman in Montana," he told Thelma.

"Like I said, she was only sixteen. I have no idea what she looks like now." She took the photograph back. "You look disappointed. You should be thankful the woman in Montana isn't Camilla. You should be very thankful."

"Were she and her brother really that bad?" he had to ask.

The old woman scoffed. "They killed their parents. Burned them to a crisp. That bad enough for you? They tried to poison me. Camilla pushed me down the stairs once no doubt hoping I would break my neck. I hate to think what they would have done if I'd broken a leg and needed the two of them to take care of me. I finally ran them off." Still clutching the photo, she sat down in a chair across from him and patted her shotgun. "I've always felt guilty about that." Her gaze came up to meet his. "But I couldn't have killed them even knowing what I was releasing on the world."

He felt a chill at her words as she looked from him to the photograph and seemed startled by what she saw.

"I grabbed the wrong photograph. This isn't Camilla. This is that awful girlfriend of Richard's." She pushed to her feet, padded out of the room and returned a moment later.

This time she handed him a photo of Richard and a girl standing on the porch outside. The girl's face was in shadow, but there was no doubt it was the woman who called herself Dee Anna Justice.

At sixteen, she already had those dark, soulless eyes.

Dee had been waiting, so she wasn't surprised when Dana finally asked.

"I know nothing about your father," Dana said, as she was making dinner. "Do you have any idea why our families separated all those years ago?"

Mary and Hank were making a huge mess building a fort in the living room. The twins were in dual high chairs spreading some awful-looking food all over themselves and anything else within reach.

Dee moved so she wasn't in their line of fire. Dana had put her to work chopping vegetables for the salad. Now she stopped to look at the small paring knife in her hand. She tried to remember exactly what she'd told Stacy.

"I really have no idea," she said, thinking that if she had to cut up one more cucumber she might start screaming. Hud hadn't been around all day. Spending "free" time with Dana and the kids was mind-numbing.

"Can you tell me what your father was like?" Dana asked as she fried chicken in a huge cast-iron skillet on the stove. The hot kitchen smelled of grease. It turned Dee's stomach.

"He was secretive," Dee said, thinking of his daughter. The real Dee Anna had never talked about her family, her father in particular, which had been fine with her because she wasn't really interested. She liked her roommates to keep to themselves, just share an apartment, not their life stories.

"Secretive?" Dana said with interest. "And your mother?"

Dee gave her the same story she'd given Stacy. She had actually met Marietta Justice, so that made it easy.

"That surprises me. I can't imagine why my family wouldn't have been delighted to have Walter marry so well," Dana said.

"Maybe they didn't want him leaving here and they knew that was exactly what was going to happen," Dee said, as she chopped the last cucumber and dumped it into the salad. The entire topic of Dee Anna's family bored her. If Dana wanted to hear about an interesting family, Dee could tell her about hers.

"Tell me more about your side of the family," Dee said, knowing Dana would jump at the chance. She tuned her out as she ripped up the lettuce the way Dana had showed her and thought about her plan. She felt rushed, but she had no choice. In order to make this happen, she had to move fast.

Hilde had done a lot of damage, but Dee was sure that after Dana and the kids were gone, Hud would lean on her. Eventually.

She thought of the man she'd met on the airplane. He was still over on the Yellowstone River for a few more days. All she had to do was pick up the phone and call him. She could walk away from here and never look back. All her instincts told her that was the thing to do.

Dee heard the kids start screaming in the other room, then the front door slam. A moment later Hud Savage came into the kitchen with Mary and Hank hanging off him like monkeys. All three were laughing.

"What smells so good?" he asked. Even the two babies got excited to see him and joined in the melee.

Dee watched him give Dana a kiss. She felt her heart swell. She'd never wanted anything more in her life than what Dana had. No matter how long it took, she would have this with Hud Savage. Only he would love her more than he'd ever loved Dana.

"So CAMILLA IS the woman you mentioned back in Montana," Thelma Peters said, and added under her breath, "God help you all."

Colt's heart was pounding. "If you know for certain that she and her brother killed their parents, why weren't they arrested?"

"No proof. Those two were cagey, way beyond their years. She was far worse than her brother. Smarter and colder. She made it look like an accident. Anyone who knew Camilla knew what had really happened out at that house the night of the fire. She fooled everyone else, making them feel sorry for her."

He thought about the way she'd worked Hud and Dana. Even himself that day on the river. Camilla Northland was a great actor. "And yet, you let them move in here."

"They were so young. I thought I could turn them around. I dragged the two of them to church." She shook her head. "It was a waste of time. The evil was too deep in her, and Richard was too dependent on her."

"Would you mind if I took this photograph?" he asked.

"Please do. For years, I've prayed never to see that face again. I've always worried that when I got old, she would come back here."

Thelma didn't have to say any more. He had a pretty good idea now of what Camilla might do to the aunt who had taken her in all those years ago.

"Do you believe in evil, Marshal?"

He didn't correct her. "I do now."

She nodded. "I assume she's already hurt people or you wouldn't be here."

He nodded, reminded that she'd gotten away with it, too. And might continue to get away with it because there was never any proof and she was very good at her lies.

"I pray you can stop her," Thelma said. "I couldn't. But maybe you can."

HILDE WAS AT the shop when Colt called. After Dana had left, she'd been so upset she'd thought about going home. But she couldn't stand the thought of her empty house. So she'd stayed and helped set up the new sewing machines with Ronnie.

When her cell phone rang, she jumped as if she'd been electrocuted. Ronnie shot her a worried look. Hilde saw that it was Colt calling and, heart racing, hurried into the break room and closed the door.

"Where are you?" she asked.

"On my way to the airport. I was able to get a flight out this afternoon. If I can make the tight connections, I'll be home tonight."

Home tonight. She thrilled at his words. "It is *so* good to hear your voice."

"Rough day?" he asked. "Hilde—"

"Don't worry, I haven't seen Dee. Dana stopped by. I'll tell you about it when you get back." She braced herself. "What did you find out?"

"First, I need you to remain calm. I almost didn't call you because I was afraid you'd go charging out to the ranch."

"She's this Camilla person who they think killed her own parents," Hilde said.

"Yes."

She closed her eyes, gripping the phone, emotions bombarding her from every direction. Relief that she'd been right about the woman. Terror since a killer was still out at the ranch with her best friend and her kids.

"Listen to me, Hilde. If you go charging out there or even call, they aren't going to believe you—and you could force Dee to do something drastic and jeopardize everyone, okay?"

She nodded to herself, knowing what he was saying was true. Dana wouldn't believe Colt any more than she had Hilde. "You've told Hud, though, right? So he's going to take care of everything."

"I've been trying to reach him. I've left him a message. He'll know how to handle this. I need your word that you'll sit tight. I'll be there by tonight and this will all be over."

She wished it were that simple. She prayed he was right. "Okay. I know what you're saying. I won't do anything."

"Where are you?"

"At the shop. I couldn't stay at the house."

"I wish you would go home and wait for me. Lock the doors. Don't leave for any reason."

She smiled, touched by his concern.

"Hilde, I…I love you."

His words brought tears of joy to her eyes. For years she'd waited for the right man to come along. Dana had been her biggest supporter.

"I want you to find someone like Hud so badly," Dana would say.

Hilde had wanted that, too, but she'd thought it could never happen.

"Are you crying?" he asked.

She gulped back a sob. This was the happiest moment of her life and she couldn't share it with her best friend. "I love you, too, Colt."

"Okay, baby," he said. "I have to go. I'll call you the moment I land. Be safe."

She hung up and let the tears fall that she'd been fighting to hold back all day.

A moment later, Ronnie opened the door a crack. "Are you all right?"

Hilde almost laughed. Dana and Hud weren't the only people looking at her strangely lately. "Colt Dawson just told me that he loves me."

Ronnie started to laugh, clearly relieved. "That's wonderful. I guess you must be one of those people who cries when they're happy?"

Hilde nodded, although some of the tears were out of a deep sadness. In a matter of days, her life had changed so drastically it made her head spin.

"Do you want me to stay with you?" Ronnie asked. "If you don't feel like locking up tonight by yourself—"

Hilde hadn't realized it was so late. "No, I'm fine."

Ronnie hesitated. Of course she'd heard about Dee's alleged attack and probably even the restraining order.

"I don't think there will be any trouble tonight," Hilde said, thinking she should have gotten a restraining order against Dee. As if a restraining order would stop someone like her.

As Ronnie left, Hilde locked up behind her. She wasn't quite ready to go home yet. A part of her was still chilled by the news that the woman posing as Dee Anna Justice was actually Camilla Northland, sister of Richard Northland, both of them believed to be cold-blooded killers.

It was easy for Hilde to believe that of Dee. She knew firsthand what the woman was capable of. The fact that Dee was probably out on the ranch right now having dinner with Dana and Hud and the kids...

Colt was right, of course. Calling out there to warn Dana was a waste of breath. It could even make matters worse.

Hilde turned out the lights in the front of the store

and walked to the break room. Closing the door, she pulled out her cell phone. At the touch of one button she could get Dana on the line.

She thought about what she could say. She hit the button. The phone rang three times. They were eating dinner. Dana wasn't going to answer the call.

Hilde had just started to hang up when it stopped ringing. "Dana?" She could hear breathing. "Dana, I just called to tell you that Colt just told me he loved me."

"I'm sorry, but you have the wrong number." The line went dead.

For just an instant, Hilde thought she had gotten the wrong number because that hadn't been Dana's voice.

Then her mind kicked into gear.

It had been Dee's voice. She'd answered Dana's cell phone.

COLT COULDN'T BELIEVE he'd blurted it out like that. *I love you.* He'd said it without thinking. He let out a chuckle. He'd just said what was in his heart.

He considered calling her back to warn her again about doing anything crazy. He had debated telling her about Dee to start with, afraid of what Hilde would do. For a woman who he suspected had never been impulsive in her life, she had been doing a lot of things on the spur of the moment lately.

Like telling him she loved him, too.

He felt his heart soar at the memory of her words. He couldn't wait to get home for so many reasons.

The moment he walked into the airport terminal, though, he felt his heart drop. Something was wrong.

He could feel it in the air as he hurried to the airline counter and saw that his flight had been canceled.

"What's going on?" he asked of a man waiting in line. He could hear a woman arguing that she had to get to Salt Lake.

"All flights into Salt Lake City have been canceled for today because of a bad spring snowstorm," the man said. "Snow's falling at a rate of six inches an hour. I just saw it on the weather channel. Doesn't look good even for in the morning."

Colt felt like the woman arguing with the airline clerk. He desperately needed to get home. But unlike that woman, he realized he wasn't going to be flying.

He'd just reached the car rental agency when Annie called from the marshal's office in Big Sky. "Ready to be surprised? Dee Anna Justice *did* book a flight to New York City for tomorrow."

He *was* surprised. "You're sure?"

"I had the airline executive double-check. Because I called concerned about Dee Anna Justice, I figure they'll take her into one of those little rooms and do an entire cavity search," she said with a satisfied chuckle.

Colt was trying to make sense of this. Dee was really leaving tomorrow? Maybe she was just covering her bets.

"Not only that, Hud announced that he plans to take Dana on a trip to Jackson Hole beginning Sunday. Jordan and Liza are going to stay at the house for a couple of days and watch the kids."

"You're sure Dee isn't going with them?" he asked.

"Definitely not. He said he hoped things calmed down once Dana put Dee on the plane."

Colt bet he did. "Thanks for doing this, Annie. One more thing. I left a message for Hud—"

"There's been a break in the burglary case in West Yellowstone. He was up there today and he's coming back tomorrow. That's probably why he hasn't returned your call."

Either that or he'd seen who'd called and didn't want to deal with his suspended deputy right now. While Hud had to be having his own misgivings about Dee, Colt knew that the marshal would be skeptical even if Colt gave him the information he'd gathered in Tuttle— until he saw the photograph of Camilla Northland and her brother.

"You're in luck," the woman behind the counter told him. "I have one vehicle left. I'm afraid it's our most expensive SUV."

"I'll take it," he said, and pulled out his credit card. Getting the paperwork done seemed to take forever. He glanced at his watch. Not quite noon. While he was waiting for the woman to finish the paperwork, he'd checked.

It was twenty-two hours to Big Sky. That didn't take into account the bad weather ahead of him. He knew he wouldn't be able to make good time once he reached the snow. He would have to make up for it when he had dry roads.

But he could reach Big Sky by late morning. He just prayed that wouldn't be too late.

Finally, she handed him the keys. A few minutes later, he was in the leather, heated-seat lap of luxury and headed north.

Hilde had sounded disappointed when he'd called to tell her the news. "But I'm glad you're on your way. Just be careful. I checked the weather before you called. It looks like that storm is going to stay to the south of us."

Neither of them had mentioned what they had said to each other earlier.

"I can't wait to see you," he said.

"Me, too."

"I'd better get off and pay attention to my driving." He'd hung up feeling all the more frustrated that he couldn't get to her more quickly. Hud still hadn't returned his call.

He pushed down on the gas pedal, hoping he didn't get pulled over.

DEE SAW HOW disappointed Dana was at dinner when Hud told her he had to go up to West Yellowstone the next day. Any other time, Dee would have felt the same way.

She touched the small vial in her pocket. Hud didn't realize how lucky he was. Now she could implement her plan without involving him. This was so much better.

"I should be back by late afternoon," Hud was saying. "What do you and Dee have planned?"

"She flies out tomorrow afternoon, so it's up to her," Dana said. She and Hud looked at Dee.

"I just want to spend the morning here on the ranch with Dana and the kids," Dee said. "I don't know when I'll get to see them again, so I want to make it last. If it's nice, I'd love to take the kids on a walk. I saw those tandem strollers you have out there. I thought we could hike up the road, pick wildflowers..."

"That's a wonderful idea," Dana said. "I could pack a lunch."

"You're not going," Dee said. "You are going to stay here and put your feet up and relax. You have been waiting on me for days. It's my turn to give you a break. The kids and I can pack the lunch, can't we?"

Mary and Hank quickly agreed. "I want peanut butter and jelly," Mary said.

"Mommy's strawberry jelly," Hank added, and Mary clapped excitedly.

"Good, it's decided," Dee said. "You aren't allowed to do any work while we're gone. When was the last time you had a chance to just relax and, say, read a book or take a nap?"

Dana smiled down the table at her, then reached to take her hand to squeeze it. "Thank you. I really am glad you came all this way to visit us. I'm just sorry—" Her eyes darkened with sadness.

"None of that," Dee said, giving her hand a squeeze back. "I can't tell you how thankful I am that you invited me."

As she sat picking at her food, the rest of the family noisily enjoying the meal, Dee counted down the hours. She could feel time slipping through her fingers, but she was relatively calm. Once she'd decided what she was going to have to do, she'd just accepted it.

She'd learned as a child to just accept things the way they were—until she could change them. There was nothing worse than feeling trapped in a situation where you felt there was nothing you could do.

That had been her childhood—feeling defenseless. She'd sworn that the day would come when she would never feel like that again. It took a steely, blind determination that some might have thought cold.

But the moment she'd lit that match so many years ago, she'd sworn she was never going to be a victim again.

Chapter Fourteen

Hud had been in such a good mood after dinner that he'd suggested one last horseback ride.

Dee couldn't contain her excitement once she'd heard that it would be just the two of them. Dana had considered calling Liza to see if she would babysit, but one of the twins was teething and cranky, so she'd told Hud and Dee to go and have a good time.

"Oh, here," Hud had said. "I picked up the mail on my way in. You had something, Dee." Mail was delivered to a large box with Cardwell Ranch stenciled on the side. The box sat at the edge of Highway 191, a good quarter mile from the ranch house.

She took the envelope with the name Dee Anna Justice typed on it. The trust fund check. She hoped she would never have to use it. But it was always good to have money tucked away—just in case she had reason to leave town in a hurry.

Hud watched her open it, peek inside, then stuff the folded envelope into the hip pocket of her jeans. Having mail come to her in Dee Anna Justice's name seemed to seal the deal as far as who she was. At least for Hud.

While he went out to saddle two horses, Dee insisted on staying in the house and helping Dana with the dishes. She could tell Hud had liked that.

Hud smiled at her now as she walked out to the corral where he was waiting. She smiled back, warmed to her toes. He seemed comfortable and at ease with her. She wouldn't let herself think that his good mood had to do with her plans to fly out the next day.

It was the perfect evening, the weather cool but not cold. The sky was still bright over the canyon, the sun not yet set.

Dee let him help her into the saddle, loving being this close to him. She felt comfortable in the saddle. Hud could never love a woman who didn't ride.

"I think I could get into horseback riding," she said, as the two of them left the ranch behind and headed up into the mountains.

"You should check into riding lessons when you get home," he suggested. "I'm sure they're offered in New York."

"Yes," she agreed, reminded again that there was nothing waiting for her back in the city. She'd given up the apartment. Given up that life.

She considered what the real Dee Anna Justice would do once she realized Dee had borrowed her name. The best thing to do was send the check back. Put "Wrong Address" on the envelope. Dee Anna would never have to know.

That decided, Dee began to relax and enjoy the ride and the man riding along next to her. At that moment she was so content, so sure that everything was going to work out the way she'd planned it, that she couldn't have foreseen the mistake she would make just minutes later on top of the mountain.

COLT MADE GOOD time, and by seven that night he wasn't far outside Denver. He stopped for gas and coffee, figuring he had at least another fourteen hours minimum to go.

Hilde answered on the second ring as if she'd been waiting by the phone. "Where are you?"

He told her. "The roads haven't been bad. I expect they will be worse the closer I get. I should be there by nine or ten in the morning. Get some sleep."

"What about you?" she asked.

"I'm okay. When I first got into law enforcement I had to work some double shifts. I learned how to stay awake. Anyway, I'll be thinking of you the whole time."

He could hear the smile in her voice when she said, "Same here."

He stretched his legs and got back into the SUV. He tried Hud again. His call went straight to voice mail. Cussing under his breath, he headed for the interstate.

His thoughts were with Hilde. What Camilla's aunt had told him had him scared.

"Even when she was a little girl, if another child had a toy she wanted, she'd take it from her," Thelma Peters had said. "If that child got hurt in the process, Camilla was all the more happy for it. I remember one time scolding her for that behavior. She must have been four or five at the time. She and her family had come for a visit. Her father was often out of work. I'll never forget the way she turned to look at me. I remember my heart lurching in my chest. I was actually frightened."

Thelma had taken a moment, as if the memory had been too strong, before she continued. "That child looked at me and said, 'She should have given the toy to me when I told her to. If she got hurt, it's her own fault. Next time, she'll give it to me when I ask for it.'"

"What about her mother and father? They must have seen this kind of behavior and tried to do something about it."

Thelma had shook her head sadly. "I mentioned what I'd seen to my sister. Cynthia wasn't a strong woman. She said to me, 'Leave her be. Camilla's just a child.' Herbert? He smacked her around, then would hold her on his lap and pet her like she was a dog." The aunt had wrinkled her mouth in disgust. "That child worked him. Cynthia was too weak to stand up to her husband or her daughter."

"And Richard?"

"He idolized his sister, did whatever she wanted. The two were inseparable. I'm not surprised they were together in Montana when he died."

"There's a chance she killed him," he'd told her.

Thelma's hand had gone to her heart. "It is as if something is missing in her DNA. A caring gene. Camilla has no compassion for anyone but herself. I always wondered what she would do with Richard when she got tired of him."

"If she was responsible, why did she want her parents dead?"

Thelma had looked away. "I have my suspicions, ones I've never voiced to anyone."

"You think Herbert was abusing her?"

Her face had filled with shame. "I tried to talk to my

sister. I even called Social Services. Herbert swore it wasn't true. So did Camilla."

"You think your sister knew and just turned a blind eye."

"That's why Camilla killed them both," Thelma had said. "I saw that girl right after the police called and told me about the fire and that my sister and brother-in-law were dead. Richard? He's crying his eyes out. Camilla? Cool as a cucumber. She waltzes into the house and asks me what I have to eat, that she's starving. She sat there eating, smiling to herself. I tried to tell myself that we all grieve in our own way. But it was enough to turn my blood to ice."

As THE SUN sank lower behind the adjacent mountains, Dee and Hud reached a spot where aspens grew thick and green.

They reined in and climbed off their horses to walk to the edge of the mountain. This view was even more spectacular than the one she'd seen on the four-wheeler ride into the mountains.

"It's so peaceful here," Dee said, as she breathed in the evening. The air was scented with pine and the smell of spring. She hugged herself against the cool breeze that whispered through the trees. Shadows had puddled under them.

Unconsciously, she stepped closer to Hud as she thought of the bears and mountain lions that lived in these mountains. Hud seemed so unafraid of anything. She loved his quiet strength and wondered what her life would have been like if she'd had a father like him. Or even a brother like him.

As she glanced at him, she told herself that life had given her another chance to have such a man to protect her.

"Hud." Just saying his name sent a shiver through her.

He looked over at her expectantly as if he thought she was about to say something.

She didn't think. At that moment, she felt as if she would die if she didn't kiss him. No matter what happened, it was all she told herself she would ever want.

The kiss took him by such surprise that he didn't react at first. She felt his warm lips on hers as she pressed her chest into his hard, strong one.

One of his arms came around her as if he thought she'd stumbled into him and was about to fall off the edge of the mountain.

Several seconds passed, no more, before he pushed her away, holding her at arm's length. "What the—" His eyes darkened with anger. "What was that, Dee?" he demanded.

"I...I just—" She saw the change in his expression and knew that Hilde had warned him that she was after him. He hadn't believed her—until this moment.

Hud shoved her away from him.

She felt tears burn her eyes and anger begin to boil deep in her belly. She wanted to scream at him, *Why not me? What is so wrong with me?*

Instead, she said, "I'm so sorry," and pretended to be horrified by what she'd done when, in truth, she was furious with him.

"It was all of this," she said, motioning to the view. "I

just got swept up in it and, standing next to you..." She looked away, hating him for making her feel like this.

"We should get back," he said, and turned to walk toward the horses where he'd left them ground tied by the aspens.

She tried to breathe out her fury, to act chastised, to pretend to be remorseful. It was the hardest role she'd ever played.

They rode in silence down the mountain through the now dark pines.

Dee thought about the kiss. She'd been anticipating it for days and now felt deeply disappointed. Hud had cut her to the quick. She could never forgive him.

Worse, he would now suspect that everything Hilde had said was true. Good thing she'd made that plane reservation for tomorrow. She couldn't wait to get away from here.

HILDE GOT THE text from Dana the next morning as she was starting to open the shop.

u r rght abt D Im so—

She hurriedly tried to call her friend. The phone went straight to voice mail. "Dana, call me the moment you get this."

Hilde stood inside the shop for a moment. The apparently interrupted text scared her more than she wanted to admit.

She called the sheriff's office. If Hud was home... But she was told that Hud had been called away on a case in West Yellowstone.

So Dana was alone out at the ranch with the kids... and Dee.

Colt was on his way, but she couldn't wait for him. She had to make sure Dana was all right.

Locking the shop, she headed for her vehicle, thankful Colt had changed her flat and retrieved it for her. Her mind was racing. The text had her terrified that something had happened. She drove as fast as she could to the ranch, jumping out of the SUV and running inside the house without knocking.

"Dana!" she screamed, realizing belatedly that she should have at least thought to bring a weapon. But she didn't have a gun, let alone anything close to a weapon at the house or shop other than a pair of scissors. She shuddered at the thought.

Dana appeared in the kitchen doorway looking startled. She was wearing an apron and had flour all over her hands. "What in the—"

"Are you all right?" Hilde said, rushing to her.

"I'm fine. What's wrong?"

"I got your text."

"My *text?* I didn't send you a text. In fact, I haven't been able to find my cell phone all morning."

Belatedly, Hilde remembered who'd answered Dana's cell just the afternoon before. She looked around the kitchen as that slowly sank in. Dee must still have the cell phone. Dana hadn't sent the text. But why would Dee send her a text that said she was right unless… *"Where are the kids?"*

"Hilde, you're scaring me. The kids just left with Dee for a walk up the road."

Hilde glanced around, didn't see Angus and Brick. "The twins, too?"

"She took them in the stroller to give me some time to myself this morning."

"No one is with her?" She saw the answer in her friend's face. "We have to find them. *Now.*"

"Hilde, Dee might have her problems but—"

"Colt called me from Oklahoma."

"Oklahoma? I thought he went to Denver?"

"He went down there to find out what he could about Rick. The woman you thought was Dee is his *sister,* Dana. When they were teenagers, the two of them were suspected of torching their house and killing their parents, but it could never be proven."

Dana paled. "Dee is Rick's *sister?*"

"Her name isn't Dee Anna Justice. It's Camilla Northland. Or at least it was."

"Then where is Dee Anna Justice?"

"I have no idea, but right now we have to get the kids." For all Hilde knew, the woman calling herself Dee had killed Dana's cousin and taken over her life.

"You can't really believe she'd hurt my—"

"*She wants Hud, Dana.* She's been after your life since the moment she saw Hud. Do you really think she wants the kids as well?"

Dana seemed to come out of the trance Dee'd had her in since arriving in Montana. Surely she'd seen the way Dee fawned over her husband.

"Hud told me she has a crush on him, but… You *have* to be wrong about her," Dana cried. But she grabbed the shotgun she kept high on the wall by the back door.

As they ran outside, Hilde prayed the babies were all right. She told herself that if Dee stood any chance of getting away with this, then she couldn't have hurt them. But the woman had apparently already gotten away with murdering her own parents—and her brother. Possibly Dana's cousin as well. Who knew what she'd do to get what she wanted.

Dee and the kids were nowhere in sight.

"She must have gone up the road," Dana said.

"There!" Hilde cried as she spotted the stroller lying on its side in front of the barn. Dana rushed into the barn first, Hilde right behind her. They both stopped, both breathing hard.

"Mary! Hank!" Dana called, her voice breaking. Silence. She called again, her voice more frantic.

A faint cry came from one of the stalls.

Rushing toward it, they found Mary and Hank holding the twins in the back of the stall. Hilde heard the relief rush from Dana as she dropped to the straw.

"What are you two doing?" Hilde asked, fear making her voice tight.

"We're playing a game," Hank said.

"Auntie Dee told us to stay here and not make a sound," Mary said in a conspiratorial whisper.

"But Mary made a sound when she heard you calling for her," Hank said. "Now Auntie Dee is going to be mad, and when she's mad she's kind of scary."

"Where is Auntie Dee?" Hilde asked.

Hank shook his head and seemed to see the shotgun his mother had rushed in with. "Are you and Auntie Hilde going hunting?"

"We are," Hilde said. "That's why we need you and your sister to stay here and keep playing the game for just a little longer. Can you do that?"

Dana shot her friend a look, then picked up the shotgun. "Be very quiet. We'll be back in just a minute, okay?" Both children nodded and touched fingers to their lips.

Hilde stepped out of the stall and looked down the line of stalls. The light was dim and cool in the huge barn. Dee could be anywhere.

As they moved away from the stall with the children inside, Dana whispered, "Maybe it *is* just a game."

Hilde bit back a curse. Dana was determined to see the best in everyone—especially this cousin who'd ingratiated herself into their lives. But Hilde had to admit whatever game Camilla Northland was playing, it didn't make any sense.

They both jumped when they heard the barn door they'd come through slam shut. An instant later, they heard the board that locked it closed come down with a heart-stopping thud.

"She just locked us in," Hilde said, her voice breaking.

Dana had already turned and was racing toward the back door of the barn. Hilde knew before she saw Dana reach it that she would find it locked.

Only moments later did she smell the smoke.

Chapter Fifteen

"I'm about ten minutes outside of Big Sky," Colt said when he'd called Hilde's phone and gotten voice mail. "I don't know where you are or why you aren't picking up." He didn't know what else to say so he disconnected and tried to call her at the shop.

His anxiety grew when the recording came on giving the shop's hours. He glanced at his watch. Hilde was a stickler for punctuality. If she'd gone to the shop, there was no way she would be thirty minutes late for work unless something was wrong.

When his phone rang, he thought it was Hilde. Prayed it was. He didn't even look to see who was calling and was surprised when he heard Hud's voice.

"I can't get into all of it right now," he told Hud, "but I have proof the woman at the ranch isn't Dee Anna Justice, and I can't reach Hilde at the shop or on her cell. I can't reach the ranch, either."

"I'm on my way home from West Yellowstone," Hud said. "I haven't been able to reach Dana, either. I was hoping you had heard something."

"I'm five minutes out," Colt said. "I'm going straight to the ranch."

"I'm twenty minutes out. Call me as soon as you know something."

He hung up and called the office, asked if there was any backup, but Deputy Liza Turner Cardwell was in Bozeman testifying in a court case and Deputy Jake Thorton was up in the mountains fishing on his day off.

"Liza should be back soon," Annie had told him.

Not soon enough, he feared. He tried Dana's brother Jordan. No answer. No surprise. Jordan was busy building his house and probably out peeling logs.

He disconnected as he came up behind a semi, laid on his horn and swore. The driver slowed, but couldn't find a place to pull over and the road had too many blind curves to pass.

Colt felt a growing sense of urgency. He needed to get to Cardwell Ranch. *Now.* All his instincts told him that Hilde was there and in trouble. Which meant so were Dana and the kids.

Mentally, he kicked himself as the vehicles in both lanes finally pulled over enough to let him through. He shouldn't have told Hilde what he found out in Oklahoma. She must have gone out to the ranch to warn Dana. He wouldn't let himself imagine what the woman calling herself Dee Anna Justice would do if cornered.

ALONG WITH THE smell of smoke, Hilde caught the sharp scent of fuel oil. She could hear the crackling of flames. The barn was old, the wood dry. Past the sound of fire they heard an engine start up.

For just an instant Hilde thought Dee might be planning to save them—the way she had her at the falls and possibly the way she had tried on the river.

But they heard the pickup leave, the sound dying off as the flames grew louder.

They rushed back to the children. Hilde dug in her pocket for her cell phone, belatedly realizing she'd left it in the SUV when she'd jumped out. She looked up at Dana. "You said you haven't been able to find your cell phone?"

Dana shook her head. The smoke was getting thicker inside the barn. Hilde could see flames blackening the kindling dry wood on all sides. It wouldn't be long before the whole barn was ablaze.

"Let's try to break through the side of the barn," Hilde said, grabbing up a shovel. She began to pound at the old wood. It splintered but the boards held.

Dana joined her with another shovel.

Hilde couldn't believe Dee thought she could get away with this. But at the back of her mind, she feared Dee would. Somehow, she would slip out of this, the same way she had as a kid. The same way she had killed her brother and gone free. And it would be too late for Hilde and Dana and the kids.

"I can't believe she would hurt innocent children," Dana said, tears in her eyes.

"What's wrong, Mommy?" Mary asked.

"Is the barn on fire?" Hank asked.

Hilde and Dana kept pounding at the wood at the back of the stall. If she could just make a hole large enough for the kids to climb out.

The wood finally gave way. She and Dana grabbed hold of the board and were able to break it off to form a small hole. Not large enough for them, but definitely large enough to get the children out.

What would happen to them if Dee saw them, though? They'd heard the sound of the pickup engine, but what if she hadn't really left? The question passed silently between the two friends.

"We're going to play another game," Dana said, crouching down next to Mary and Hank. "You and your sister are going to crawl out. I am going to hand you Angus and Brick. Then you're going to go hide in that outbuilding where we keep the old tractor. You can't let Dee see you, okay?"

Hank nodded. "We'll sneak along the haystack. No one will see us."

"Good boy," Dana said, her voice breaking with emotion. "Take care of the babies until either me or Daddy calls you. Don't make a sound if Dee calls you, okay? Now hurry."

Hilde looked out through the hole. No sign of Dee. She helped Hank out and Dana handed him Angus. Mary crawled out next and took Brick. They quickly disappeared from sight.

The smoke was thick now, the flames licking closer and closer as the whole barn went up in flames.

"Oh, Hilde, I'm so sorry for not trusting you," Dana cried, and hugged her.

"Right now, we have to find a way out of here."

The two of them tried to find another spot along the wall where they could get out. The barn was old but sturdily built, and the smoke was so thick now that staying low wasn't helping. They could hear the flames growing closer and closer.

With a *whoosh* the back of the barn began to cave in. The rest of the structure groaned and creaked. But over the roar of the flames and the falling boards, Hilde heard another sound. A vehicle headed in their direction.

DEE HAD LEFT Dana a note. "I couldn't find you and the kids when I got ready to leave for the airport, so I borrowed your pickup. Thank you for everything. I'll leave the truck in long-term parking. Dee."

Then she'd taken the keys from where she'd seen Dana hang them on a hook by the door and left.

After they'd finished their horseback ride yesterday, Hud had unsaddled the horses and put everything away. Then she'd heard him go upstairs, his boots heavy on the steps, as if he dreaded telling his wife about her cousin.

She'd listened hard but hadn't heard a sound once he entered his and Dana's bedroom, confirming what she'd suspected. That he hadn't awakened Dana last night to tell her.

Earlier this morning when Dee had come downstairs, she'd seen Hud and Dana with their heads together. He had definitely told her something. She'd seen how reluctant he was to leave his wife. They'd done their best to act normal. But she could tell they were counting down the hours until she left.

She'd helped herself to a cup of coffee. Dana had made French toast and sausage for breakfast and offered her a plate. Dee ate heartily as Dana took care of the kids and nibbled at the food on her plate. "You should eat more breakfast," Dee told her.

"I'm fine. Anyway, I still need to lose a few pounds after the twins."

But this is your last breakfast, Dee had wanted to say. She hoped on her last day on earth she ate a good breakfast, since she would never be eating again.

As she drove away from the ranch, she glanced at the barn. Flames were licking up the sides. She looked away, thinking how sad it was that things hadn't worked out differently.

She looked back only once more as she drove past Big Sky. Smoke billowed up into the air across the river, an orange glow behind the pines. She gave the pickup more gas. She had a plane to catch, and there was no going back and changing things now.

She turned on the radio and began to sing along. She had no idea where she was going or what she would do when she got there, but she had Dee Anna Justice's trust fund check and options. She would find another identity and disappear.

What amazed her as she left the canyon was that she'd ever thought she could be happy living on Cardwell Ranch with Hud.

COLT SAW THE smoke and flames in the distance the moment he came out of the narrow part of the canyon. He felt his heart drop. He raced up the highway, calling the fire department as he went, and turned onto the ranch road.

At first he thought it was the house on fire, but as he came up over a rise, he saw that it was the barn. For a moment he felt a wave of relief. Then he saw Hilde's SUV parked in front of the house. Dana's ranch pickup was gone. Maybe they'd all left to take Dee to the airport. Maybe they were all fine.

But his gut told him differently.

When he saw the stroller lying on its side in front of the barn and the door barred, he knew. Holding his hand down on the horn, he hit the gas and raced toward the burning front door of the barn.

The bumper smashed through the burning wood as the expensive rental SUV burst into the barn. Pieces of burning wood hit the windshield, sparks flew all around him and then there was nothing but dark thick smoke.

The moment the SUV broke through the door, he hit his brakes. *It's too late,* he thought when he saw the entire shell of the barn in flames, the smoke so thick he couldn't see his hand in front of his face. He leaped from the rig, screaming Hilde's name. The heat was so intense he felt as if his face were burning. He feared the vehicle's gas tank would explode any moment.

Then he heard her answer.

She and Dana came out of the smoky darkness silhouetted against the walls of flames.

"Where are the babies?" he yelled over the roar of the flames.

"They got out!" Hilde yelled back.

He shoved them both into the SUV and threw it in Reverse. The heat was unbearable. He knew if he didn't get the rig out now…

The hood of the SUV, the paint peeling and blackened, had just cleared the edge of the barn when he heard the loud crash, and the barn began to collapse.

If he'd been just a few minutes later…

He wouldn't let himself even imagine that as he slammed on the brakes back from the inferno. Hilde and Dana were coughing and choking, but he could hear fire trucks and the ambulance on its way.

"My babies," Dana choked out.

"They're in that outbuilding," Hilde said, pointing a good ways from the burning remains of the barn.

"Where's Dee?" he asked them.

"She left after she started the fire," Hilde said.

"I heard her take my truck," Dana added. She was already getting out of the SUV to go after her children, Hilde at her heels. Colt ran ahead and found the children all safe, huddled together in a back corner of the outbuilding.

Later, as the fire department and EMTs took care of Hilde and Dana and the kids, he told Hilde, "I have to go after Dee. I can't let her get on that plane."

"I'm fine," she told him. "Go!"

Chapter Sixteen

The ride to the airport outside of Bozeman was the longest one of Colt's life. He called ahead and asked that Dee Anna Justice be detained, but he was told that she'd already gone through security. Two airport officials were looking for her, but so far they hadn't found anyone matching the description he'd given them.

Camilla's plane was scheduled to board within twenty minutes.

"Don't let her get on that plane," Colt ordered. "Hold her there until I get there. Consider her armed and dangerous."

"Armed? She just went through security. I'm sure if she was—"

"You don't know this woman. She's dangerous. Have your officers approach her with extreme caution."

He was just outside of Belgrade when Hud called.

"I'm on my way to the airport," Hud said. "Make sure that woman doesn't get away, Deputy."

"I'm doing my best," Colt said. "But I'm on suspension."

"Your suspension was lifted hours ago," Hud said. "About the time you saved my wife's life. We'll talk about that later. Where are you?"

Colt told him he was turning onto the airport road. He was only minutes away from confronting Camilla Northland.

DEE LOOKED INTO the women's restroom mirror, appraising herself. She'd brushed out her hair. Since it was naturally curly, it flowed around her head like a dark halo.

She'd applied makeup, especially eye shadow, mascara and blush, sculpting her face. It amazed her how different she looked from the woman who'd been staying at Cardwell Ranch.

As she studied herself in the mirror, she liked what she saw. She'd been able to cover most of the damage she'd done to herself. But maybe when she got wherever she was going, she'd change her hair. Something short and blond. Yes, she liked that idea. A whole new her.

That thought made her laugh. When she'd first left Oklahoma, she'd believed in her heart that she could put the past behind her, become whoever and whatever she wanted.

She hadn't realized then how deep the past had embedded itself in her. It ate at her like a parasite, a constant reminder that she was broken and while she might be able to put back the pieces, she would never be whole.

One of the female security guards stuck her head in the restroom door. Camilla saw her out of the corner of her eye but continued to carefully apply another coat of bright red lipstick.

"Excuse me," the woman said. "We're checking boarding passes. May I see yours?"

"Of course," Camilla said. She took her time putting the lipstick back into her purse. "Here it is."

The woman started to take it, her attention on the slip of paper. More important the *name* on the paper. No Dee Anna Justice but Amy Matthews.

Dee Anna's boarding pass was buried at the botton of the trash container.

The security officer looked from the boarding pass to Camilla, then handed the paper back. "Have a nice flight, Ms. Matthews. I believe your flight is boarding now," the woman said.

"Thank you." Camilla walked out and got into line for the flight to Seattle. In a few minutes she would be on board.

She had hoped to catch an earlier flight, but it hadn't worked out. Fortunately, she'd planned for this, making several flights in three different names. One in the name of Dee Anna Justice to New York. Another as Amy Matthews to Seattle. And a third flight earlier that day to Las Vegas under the name Patricia Barnes.

Like Rick, she had three different identities ready. She'd just been smart enough not to get caught with them on her, though.

She'd missed the flight to Vegas by only minutes. Finishing up her business at the ranch had taken longer than she'd hoped.

Not that it mattered now. Within minutes she would be on her way to Seattle. No one was looking for Amy Matthews.

She figured Hud must have come home sooner than expected. Or that deputy, Colt Dawson, had showed up. Either way, it would be too late.

It wasn't as if she'd thought for a moment they

wouldn't suspect her given everything that had happened. But they had no proof.

Anyway, she would be long gone before they could get to the airport. Even if they should somehow track her down, they still couldn't do anything except get her for using an alias. Or yes, and pretending to be Dee Anna Justice.

She'd cried her way out of more of those situations than she could remember. If tears didn't work, then her life story definitely did. Of course she was messed up. Imagine living your life with such suspicions hanging over you.

It had worked every other time. It would now, too, because without proof, they couldn't touch her. With Dana, Hilde and the kids gone...

She left the restroom and walked to her gate. The woman taking her boarding pass told her to hurry, her flight was about to leave.

She hurried down the ramp and into the plane just moments before the flight attendant was about to shut the door. She'd timed it close, but she hadn't wanted to risk sitting at the gate in case anyone she knew was looking for her.

As she slipped into her first-class seat next to a businessman in a nice suit, she told herself her luck might be changing.

"Hello," she said and extended her hand. "I'm Amy Matthews."

"Clark Evans."

The flight attendant asked her what she would like to drink.

"I'd love a vodka Collins," she said. "I'm celebrating.

Today's my birthday. Join me?" she asked the business executive, taking in his gold cuff links, the cut of his suit and the expensive wristwatch.

"How can I say no?" he said, already flirting with her.

"Yes, how can you?" she asked, flirting back. "I have a feeling that this could be a very interesting flight."

COLT RAN INTO the airport. The head of security met him the moment he came through the door.

"Dee Anna Justice hasn't checked in for her flight. It was supposed to leave ten minutes ago," the man told him. "We've held it as long as we can. So far, she's a no-show."

"Dee Anna Justice definitely isn't on the flight? You checked all the passengers?"

"No one matching her description is on the flight, and everyone is accounted for," he assured Colt.

Colt had been so sure she would make her flight. As gutsy as the woman was and as bulletproof as she'd been, she would think she had nothing to fear.

She'd already gone through security, so she'd been here. But that didn't mean she didn't change her mind and leave.

Maybe she was running scared, though he highly doubted it. Camilla had an arrogance born of getting away with murder.

"What other flights have left in the last hour?" he asked.

"Only one, but it's to Seattle. The plane is taxiing down the runway right now."

"Stop that plane."

"I'm not sure—"

"This woman just tried to kill six people, four of them children, by burning them alive. Stop the plane. *Now*."

CAMILLA WAS SIPPING her drink, smiling at her companion, when the pilot announced they would be returning to the terminal because of an instrument malfunction.

She looked past the man next to her out his window. Sunlight ricocheted off the windows of the terminal, reminding her of the day she'd flown in here. If she'd gone fishing on the Yellowstone River with Lance...

Still, even though she knew there was nothing wrong with the instruments, she wasn't worried. The barn had been burning so quickly, the boards locking the doors would be ashes—all evidence gone.

Even the spilled fuel oil she'd used to get the barn burning fast would look like nothing more than an accident—at first. She'd started the fire with several candles she'd found in the back of Hilde's sewing shop, complete with the cute little quilted mats that went with them.

Everyone knew that Hilde had been losing her mind lately. But to do something this horrible because Dana turned against her? It was almost unthinkable—unless her behavior had been so out of character lately that everyone feared she was having a nervous breakdown. But taking her own life and her friend's along with Dana's four children? This story would make headlines across the country.

The plane taxied back to the small terminal. It wasn't but a few minutes after she'd heard the door being opened that Deputy Colt Dawson appeared.

She turned to the man next to her and asked him a question. Out of the corner of her eye, she saw Colt start to move through the plane. He was almost past her when he stopped and took a step back until he was right at her elbow. "Camilla," he said.

She looked up at him, frowned and said, "I'm sorry. You're mistaken. My name is Amy Matthews."

"Miss...Matthews. I'd like you to come with me. *Now,*" he said when she hesitated. "You won't be taking this flight today."

She sighed and, picking up her bag, got to her feet. "We'll have to celebrate another time," she told the businessman. Colt took her bag from her and quickly frisked her, which made her smile as if she was amused.

"I never noticed how cute you are," she said, as he escorted her off the plane to four waiting security guards. He insisted on cuffing her once she was out of sight of the passengers.

"Is that really necessary?" she asked. "What is this about, anyway? So I didn't use my real name. I have an old boyfriend who I don't want to find me. So sue me."

"This is about the attempted murder of six individuals, four of them children." Colt appeared to be fighting to keep his emotions in check.

Camilla was silent for a moment, then she frowned and said, "Attempted?"

"That's right. They're all alive. Hilde and Dana will be testifying against you in court."

Camilla let out a little laugh. "I suppose you're the one I should thank for this?"

"Be my guest," Colt said, as he led her up the ramp.

They were almost to the boarding area when Marshal Hud Savage appeared.

Colt felt Camilla tense. They all did at the look in the marshal's eyes. Colt knew exactly how he felt. In the old West she would have been strung up from the nearest tree.

But this wasn't the old West, and he and Hud didn't mete out justice. All they could do was hope and pray that this woman never saw the outside of a cell for the rest of her life.

ONCE AT THE law enforcement center, Camilla Northland's story was that she'd left the ranch right after Hilde arrived. Dana was with the kids on the front porch as she drove away and had asked Hilde if she wanted to go on a walk with them. That was the last she said that she saw of them.

She'd seemed surprised that Dana and Hilde had told another story. "I don't know why they would lie, except that Hilde has been telling lies about me ever since I came to Montana, and Dana must be confused."

"It's over, Camilla," Colt said, as they all sat in the interrogation room. He tossed the photo of her as a teenager on the table. "Your aunt told me everything. She said she would fly up here if need be."

She stared at the photo of herself and her brother. When she looked up, she suddenly looked tired—and almost relieved.

"It would appear I'm going to need a lawyer," she said.

"Just tell me this. How was it that you ended up here pretending to be Dee Anna Justice?"

For a moment, she didn't look as if she would answer. "Dee Anna was my roommate in New York City for a while," she said with a shrug. "The letter came after she'd moved out."

"And you decided to take her identity?"

"I'd never been to Montana," she said. "I liked the idea of having a cousin I'd never met." She looked unapologetic as her gaze locked with Hud's. "And I'd never met a real cowboy."

"Where is Dee Anna Justice?" Hud demanded, clearly not amused by her flirting with him.

She looked away for a moment, and Colt felt his heart drop. He now knew what extremes this woman would go to and feared for the real Dee Anna Justice.

"She's in Spain visiting some friend of hers. Her mother, Marietta, probably knows how to contact her."

"Marietta's family is from Spain?"

"Italy." Camilla smiled. "No one told you that Dee Anna is half-Italian?" She laughed. "Dana asked me why her grandparents disinherited their son. He married a *foreigner.* Apparently a woman who spoke Italian and wanted to live in the big city wasn't what they wanted for their son. But you'd have to ask Dee Anna if that is really why they disinherited him." She shrugged. "Dee Anna and I were never close. She was a lot like Hilde. For some reason, she didn't like me." Camilla laughed at that. "I'll take that lawyer now."

Epilogue

Hilde held it all together until a few weeks after Camilla's arrest. Suddenly she was bombarded with so many emotions that she finally let herself cry as the ramifications of what had happened—and what had almost happened—finally hit her.

Over it all was a prevailing sadness. She and Dana were trying to repair their relationship, but Hilde knew it would take time—and never be the same. She felt as if someone had died and that made her all the sadder.

"Hilde, can you ever forgive me?" Dana had cried that day, as they'd watched the rest of the barn burn from the back of the ambulance. "I should have listened to you. I'm so sorry. I'm just so sorry."

"There is nothing to forgive," she'd told Dana, as they'd hugged. But in her heart, she knew that something was broken. Only time would tell if it could be fixed.

Hud was going through something even worse, Colt had told her. He blamed himself for not seeing what was right in front of his eyes.

"I was just so happy that Dana was enjoying her cousin, I made excuses for Dee's behavior just like Dana did. I didn't want to see it," he kept saying. "I almost lost my family because of it. And what I did to Hilde—"

She'd told him and Dana both that she understood. Camilla had been too good at hiding her true self. Hilde didn't blame them. But a part of her was disappointed in them that they hadn't believed her—the friend they'd both known for years. That was going to be the hard part to repair in the friendship.

Colt was wonderful throughout it all. He'd saved her life and Dana's. Neither of them would ever forget that.

Hilde, who'd always thought of herself as strong, had leaned on him, needing his quiet strength to see her through. Both she and Dana had recovered from the smoke inhalation. It was the trauma of being trapped in a burning barn with a psychopath trying to kill them that had residual effects.

Jordan and Liza had a housewarming a few months after everything settled down. Their new home was beautiful, and Hilde could see the pride they shared with all the work they'd done themselves. Hilde gave them a quilt as a housewarming present.

"I'd like to take your beginner quilting class," Liza said, making both Hilde and Dana look at her in surprise. She was a tomboy like Dana and had never sewn a thing in her life.

Liza grinned and looked over at Jordan, who nodded. "We're going to have a baby! I want to make her a baby quilt."

Cheers went up all around, and Hilde said she would be delighted to teach her to quilt, and she also had some adorable baby quilt patterns for girls.

"Stop by the shop and I'll show you," she said.

AT THE PARTY, Dana told Hilde that she'd called Marietta Justice, only to receive a return call from the woman's assistant confirming that the real Dee Anna Justice was alive and well in Spain traveling with friends.

Hilde could tell that Dana had been disappointed the woman hadn't even bothered to talk to her herself. But fortunately, Dana hadn't taken it any further. Whatever was going on in that part of the Justice family, it would remain a mystery.

At least for now, since Hilde knew her friend too well. Dana had a cousin she'd never met. Maybe more than one. She wouldn't forget about the very real and mysterious Dee Anna Justice and family. One of these days, Dana wouldn't be able to help herself and she would contact her cousin.

Hilde hated to think what might happen—but then again, she wasn't as trusting as Dana, was she?

The party was fun, even though things were still awkward between all of them.

"THEY'LL GET BETTER," Colt promised her. "You and the Savages were too good of friends before this happened. Right now everyone is a little bruised and battered, especially you. I can see how badly they both feel when they're around you."

That was what was making things so awkward. They wore their regrets on their sleeves.

"Are you still worried about Hud?" she asked him on their way back to her house.

"He's really beating himself up. I think he's questioning whether he should remain marshal. He's afraid he can't trust his judgment."

"That's crazy. He's a great marshal."

"He let a psychopath not only live with them, but also take his children for a walk the morning of the fire."

"He didn't know she was a psychopath."

"Yeah. I think that's the point. He overlooked so much because he wanted Dana to have a good time with her cousin. You told me how excited she was about finding a cousin she'd never met."

Hilde nodded. "They both tried to make the woman he thought was Dee Anna Justice fit into their family. Dana was at odds with her siblings for years, so I understand her need for family."

Colt looked over at her. "What about you?"

"Me?"

"How do you feel about a large family?"

She laughed. "As an only child, I've always yearned for one."

"Good," he said with a smile. "Because I have a large family up north, and they're all anxious to meet you."

She looked at him. "You want me to meet your family?"

He slowed the truck, stopping on a small rise. In the distance, Lone Mountain was silhouetted against Montana's Big Sky. Stars glittered over it. A cool breeze came in through his open window, smelling of the river and the dense pines. The summer night was perfect.

Colt cut the engine and turned toward her. "I can't wait for my family to meet you. I'm just hoping I can introduce you as my fiancée."

Hilde caught her breath as he reached into his pocket and pulled out a small black jewelry box.

"Hilde Jacobson? Will you marry me?" He opened the box, and the perfect emerald-cut diamond caught in the starlight.

For a moment she couldn't speak. So much had happened, and yet they'd all come out of the ashes alive with their futures ahead of them.

"I know this is sudden, but we can have a long engagement if that's what you want," Colt added when she didn't answer him.

She shook her head. She'd always been a woman who never acted impulsively. Until recently. She believed in taking her time on any decision she made. Especially the huge ones.

But if she'd learned anything from all this, it was that she had to follow her instincts—and her heart. "I would love to marry you, Colt Dawson. I can't wait to be your bride."

He let out a relieved laugh and slipped the ring on her finger. It fit perfectly. As he pulled her into his arms and kissed her, Lone Mountain glowed in the starlight.

"I was so hoping you would say that," he whispered.

Wrapped in his arms, she knew whatever the future held, they would face it together. Time and love were powerful healers. With Colt by her side, she could do anything, she thought, as her heart filled to overflowing.

* * * * *

COMING NEXT MONTH from Harlequin® Intrigue®
AVAILABLE APRIL 23, 2013

#1419 THE MARSHAL'S HOSTAGE
The Marshals of Maverick County
Delores Fossen
Marshal Dallas Walker is none too happy to learn his old flame, Joelle Tate, is reopening a cold case where he is one of her prime suspects.

#1420 SPECIAL FORCES FATHER
The Delancey Dynasty
Mallory Kane
A Special Forces operative and a gutsy psychiatrist must grapple with a ruthless kidnapper—and their unflagging mutual attraction—to save the child she never wanted him to know about.

#1421 THE PERFECT BRIDE
Sutton Hall Weddings
Kerry Connor
To uncover the truth about her friend's death, Jillian Jones goes undercover as a bride-to-be at a mysterious mansion, soon drawing the suspicions of the manor's darkly handsome owner—and the attention of a killer....

#1422 EXPLOSIVE ATTRACTION
Lena Diaz
A serial bomber fixates on Dr. Darby Steele and only police detective Rafe Morgan can help her. Together they try to figure out how she became the obsession of a madman before she becomes the next victim.

#1423 PROTECTING THEIR CHILD
Angi Morgan
Texas Ranger Cord McCrea must escape through the west Texas mountains with his pregnant ex-wife to stay one step ahead of the deadly gunman who has targeted his entire family.

#1424 BODYGUARD LOCKDOWN
Donna Young
Booker McKnight has sworn revenge on the man who killed fifty men—Booker's men. His bait? The only woman he's ever loved. The problem? She doesn't know.

You can find more information on upcoming Harlequin® titles, free excerpts and more at www.Harlequin.com.

HICNM0413

REQUEST YOUR FREE BOOKS!
2 FREE NOVELS PLUS 2 FREE GIFTS!

INTRIGUE

BREATHTAKING ROMANTIC SUSPENSE

YES! Please send me 2 FREE Harlequin Intrigue® novels and my 2 FREE gifts (gifts are worth about $10). After receiving them, if I don't wish to receive any more books, I can return the shipping statement marked "cancel." If I don't cancel, I will receive 6 brand-new novels every month and be billed just $4.49 per book in the U.S. or $5.24 per book in Canada. That's a savings of at least 14% off the cover price! It's quite a bargain! Shipping and handling is just 50¢ per book in the U.S. and 75¢ per book in Canada.* I understand that accepting the 2 free books and gifts places me under no obligation to buy anything. I can always return a shipment and cancel at any time. Even if I never buy another book, the two free books and gifts are mine to keep forever.

182/382 HDN FVQV

Name	(PLEASE PRINT)	

Address		Apt. #

City	State/Prov.	Zip/Postal Code

Signature (if under 18, a parent or guardian must sign)

Mail to the **Harlequin® Reader Service:**
IN U.S.A.: P.O. Box 1867, Buffalo, NY 14240-1867
IN CANADA: P.O. Box 609, Fort Erie, Ontario L2A 5X3
**Are you a subscriber to Harlequin Intrigue books
and want to receive the larger-print edition?
Call 1-800-873-8635 or visit www.ReaderService.com.**

* Terms and prices subject to change without notice. Prices do not include applicable taxes. Sales tax applicable in N.Y. Canadian residents will be charged applicable taxes. Offer not valid in Quebec. This offer is limited to one order per household. Not valid for current subscribers to Harlequin Intrigue books. All orders subject to credit approval. Credit or debit balances in a customer's account(s) may be offset by any other outstanding balance owed by or to the customer. Please allow 4 to 6 weeks for delivery. Offer available while quantities last.

Your Privacy—The Harlequin® Reader Service is committed to protecting your privacy. Our Privacy Policy is available online at www.ReaderService.com or upon request from the Harlequin Reader Service.

We make a portion of our mailing list available to reputable third parties that offer products we believe may interest you. If you prefer that we not exchange your name with third parties, or if you wish to clarify or modify your communication preferences, please visit us at www.ReaderService.com/consumerschoice or write to us at Harlequin Reader Service Preference Service, P.O. Box 9062, Buffalo, NY 14269. Include your complete name and address.

SPECIAL EXCERPT FROM

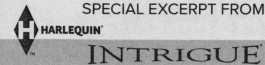

HARLEQUIN®

INTRIGUE®

THE MARSHAL'S HOSTAGE
by USA TODAY *bestselling author*
Delores Fossen

*A sexy U.S. marshal and a feisty bride-to-be must go on
the run when danger from their past resurfaces....*

"Where the hell do you think you're going?" Dallas demanded.

But he didn't wait for an answer. He hurried to her, hauled her onto his shoulder caveman-style and carried her back into the dressing room.

That's when she saw the dark green Range Rover squeal to a stop in front of the church.

Owen.

Joelle struggled to get out of Dallas's grip, but he held on and turned to see what had captured her attention. Owen, dressed in a tux, stepped from the vehicle and walked toward his men. She had only seconds now to defuse this mess.

"I have to talk to him," she insisted.

"No. You don't," Dallas disagreed.

Joelle groaned because that was the pigheaded tone she'd encountered too many times to count.

"I'll be the one to talk to Owen," Dallas informed her. "I want to find out what's going on."

Joelle managed to slide out of his grip and put her feet on the floor. She latched on to his arm to stop him from going

HIEXP0513

to the door. "You can't. You have no idea how bad things can get if you do that."

He stopped, stared at her. "Does all of this have something to do with your report to the governor?"

She blinked, but Joelle tried to let that be her only reaction. "No."

"Are you going to tell me what this is all about?" Dallas demanded.

"I can't. It's too dangerous." Joelle was ready to start begging him to leave. But she didn't have time to speak.

Dallas hooked his arm around her, lifted her and tossed her back over his shoulder.

"What are you doing?" Joelle tried to get away, tried to get back on her feet, but he held on tight.

Dallas threw open the dressing room door and started down the hall with her. "I'm kidnapping you."

Be sure to pick up
THE MARSHAL'S HOSTAGE
by USA TODAY *bestselling author Delores Fossen,*
on sale April 23 wherever
Harlequin Intrigue books are sold!

Love the Harlequin book you just read?

Your opinion matters.

Review this book on your favorite
book site, review site, blog or your own
social media properties and share
your opinion with other readers!

HARLEQUIN®

A *Romance* FOR EVERY MOOD™

Stay up-to-date on all your
romance-reading news with the
Harlequin Shopping Guide,
featuring bestselling authors, exciting new
miniseries, books to watch and more!

The newest issue will be delivered right to you
with our compliments! There are 4 each year.

Signing up is easy.

EMAIL

ShoppingGuide@Harlequin.ca

WRITE TO US

HARLEQUIN BOOKS
Attention: Customer Service Department
P.O. Box 9057, Buffalo, NY 14269-9057

OR PHONE

1-800-873-8635 in the United States
1-888-343-9777 in Canada

Please allow 4-6 weeks for delivery of the first issue by mail.